Wareham, MA

Cover and Book Design: Nauset Press
ISBN: 979-8-9859692-8-3

Did Ya Ever Wonder...

How Some Massachusetts Towns Got Named?

A REIMAGINED HISTORY

by Andy Bailey

For all those who look at life a little differently.

Table of Contents

Please Read This First

Thank you for taking the time to read this section before moving on to the stories in this book. I believe that by reading this section first it will help you understand and enjoy the nature of the stories. First, let me say right off the bat that I am not a writer, novelist, journalist, or a reporter. I have never taken any writing courses in collage or any other type of writing instruction. Therefore, you're not going to get pages upon pages of character development. No long and lengthy descriptions of persons, places, or things in this book. This is not the Great American Novel. So, what then does "History Reimagined" mean? It means that the stories within are tall tales.

These are tales that might have been told to you by your grandfather on a summer's evening sitting on the front porch. You certainly wouldn't want to listen to someone ramble on for forty-five minutes, but a five-to-ten-minute story would be entertaining while you enjoy your lemonade or adult beverage. The stories in this book are written in that vein. The tales are told, and you will have to use your imagination to fill in the blanks. Your imagination will probably work better than anything I could embellish anyway.

You may ask why I wrote this book in the first place. Well, when my children were small, we didn't have the conveniences that parents have now. No DVD screens behind the front seat headrests. No handheld video games and all the modern marvels parents have at their disposal to entertain their children today. We had to bring coloring and story books, games, and toys to hold a child's attention on long car rides. Of course, after a half an hour of that they were bored and getting antsy. One of the ways I used to keep them happy was to make up little games and stories. One of their favorites was for me to invent stories on how the cities and towns we were driving through got their names. So that explains the stories, but why make a book?

Many years later my children have grown up, and I am working as the Postmaster of South Wellfleet, Massachusetts. Many creative people like writers, singers, and college professors live in Wellfleet. One day I was talking to one of my customers, who is an author, and we began talking about the difficulty of traveling with kids in cars. She was in my age group, and without the benefit of technology, she ended up going through the same issues I went through. I told her that I used to make up stories about the names of towns to keep the kids happy. She asked to hear one and I told her. "Tell me another" she asked. After hearing the second story she wondered if I could make up a story about her town in Connecticut. I said, "Give me some time and next time you come in, I'll have one for you." When she came in again, I shared the story I had made up about her town. She liked it and suggested that I write a book of the stories. I was like, "Please, no one would be interested in that," but she insisted. I didn't really think about it too much but every time she came into the office, she would bring it up. When my clerk, who has written two children's books herself, heard about it, I was suddenly hearing it from both sides. I said that maybe when I retire and have the time, I would consider it.

Now that I have retired from the Postal Service, my clerk continued to encourage me when we met to catch up, I decided to give it a shot and write the stories for this book. So, like I said earlier, these stories aren't grand literary works of fiction. Although some of the stories have some historical facts in them, they're mostly just tall tales you might hear sitting on that front porch on a summer evening.

CHAPTER 1
Braintree

One of most unusual tales in this book is how the town of Braintree was named. Most of you know that the Pilgrims that came to America in 1620. They were not only looking for a new life but, maybe more importantly, religious freedom. The Pilgrims that arrived on the Mayflower were not the only religious group in England that were persecuted. There were many other groups that suffered the same fate as the Pilgrims.

Most of them generally believed in the same thing with some differences. Some groups had minor differences from the Pilgrims' beliefs and a few others departed largely from the norms . The Commoners, a group numbering around forty or so souls, were one of those groups that had major differences, and most of their members lived in the East End of London. Like the Pilgrims, their views on religion did not coincide with the established religious thinking of that time. The Commoners were Christian, however, their beliefs were radical compared to the other religious groups in England. But we will get to that later in the story.

The Commoners had to keep their meetings secret to avoid persecution. The East End worked for a while because it was a section of London that most good people avoided if they could. But there were periodic raids on the Commoner's meetings that increased in frequency as time went on. Because of their peculiar ways, they were not well liked by the people in the area, who would often inform on to them to the authorities. Worshiping anything other than the established religion of England could get you arrested, tortured, or worse. Life was becoming intolerable for the Commoners, so they decided to have a meeting to discuss moving somewhere else.

The story of the Pilgrims was well known in the underground religious community. However, going to the Netherlands was not an option because of the Commoner's extreme beliefs. They decided that the best bet for the group would be to follow the Pilgrims' lead and head to the new world. The Commoner's pooled money and made plans to head to America.

In April of 1623, the thirty-two members of the Commoners who decided to make the journey to the new world boarded the good ship Anne and sailed to America. Weather-wise, it was a stormy three-month journey for all, and additionally, socially so for the Commoners. Things were calm at first, but as the other passengers on the Anne got to know the members of the Commoners, the more they distanced themselves from the strange group. The Commoners' oddness and radical religious views caused the other passengers to shun them. There was also some suspicion about the disappearance of two of the passengers from the boat, but the captain blamed it on the stormy weather encountered during the voyage. The hairy eyeballs persisted, but the Commoners counted down the days awaiting their arrival at the Plymouth Colony, where they could be free to exercise their beliefs.

The Anne arrived at Plymouth Colony on July 10, 1623. After the rough journey, all were happy to be on dry land again. As they disembarked, the new arrivals were welcomed by the Governor of the colony. The Governor would soon come to regret welcoming the Commoners. After the passengers got organized, a meeting was held with the new arrivals, the Governor, and the Colony Elders. The meeting outlined the Colony rules and what was expected of the new arrivals. Additionally, they guided the passengers to an area where they could build houses to live in. Religious expectations were also communicated which sparked tensions between the Colony and the Commoners.

The Governor explained that the people were expected to behave and adhere to certain beliefs to become members of the Colony, with its attendant protections.

The Commoners felt trapped and persecuted. It was like being in England all over again. The Leader, as he was known, went back and forth with the Elders trying to negotiate an understanding with the Colonists. The Leader was the only one who spoke for the Commoners. When asked his name, he would say "Leader." The other members of the Commoners rarely ever spoke to anyone outside of their group. They spoke only amongst themselves. After some intense negotiations, the Elders of the Colony and the Leader came to an agreement. The Commoners were given land just northwest of the Colony. They could keep to themselves there, but they were expected to help in the development of the Colony. As far as religious issues, because they were all Christians, the differences in their sects could be worked out later.

The Commoners settled on the land set aside for them just outside of the Colony. They kept to themselves as much as they could. They built rudimentary group houses to live in as well as a basic building that served as a church. They reluctantly did the community chores they had agreed to contribute to the Colony. The Colonists tried to accept them, but they were suspicions of the group. The only Commoner who would speak to them was the Leader, and when he did, he was always trying to convince them that their way of worshipping God was wrong.

He would tell them they had to accept the Commoner's version of God's will. For example, any creature comforts or nice houses that the Colonists had were distractions , and that fancy churches were an abomination. The Leader would continue ranting that the only way to serve God is to live with as much simplicity as possible. And the biggest insult to serving God would be knowledge, the greatest evil in the world, the proverbial red apple between Adam and Eve that began all the troubles for humans.

In the Commoner's views, worldly knowledge creates a barrier between the individual and God, subverting obedience to His will. Thinking leads to questioning, and questioning corrupts all pure love for God. The Commoners viewed knowledge as the sinful and rotting root of evil. To prevent temptation, the group must follow the Leader. After all, the Leader is the direct intermediary between the Commoners and God. The penalties were severe for any Commoners who broke the rules set by the leader: no thinking, no talking to outsiders, and unquestioning obedience to God.

The embers of discontent and mistrust between the Colonists and the Commoners burned for about a year. Minor annoyances and problems between the two began to escalate. There were missed community work assignments, some physical altercations, weird behavior by the Commoners, and strange noises coming from the Commoner's church at night. The constant badgering and proselytizing aimed at the Colonists by the Leader convinced four of the less thoughtful members of the Colonists to join the Commoners. Despite many meetings between the Colony Elders and the Leader, the friction between the two could not be resolved, and, in fact, worsened. The Commoners seemed to have no intention of integrating with the others to form a better community. They were hard set in their views, and there was no compromise to be had. The low-banked embers began to flare into a hot fire. Resentments started to boil over.

What finally put the situation between the Colonists and the Commoners over the edge was the horrifying discovery of a severed head hanging from a tree just outside of the Commoner's camp. One of the men from the Colony was hunting when he came upon the severed head. He went back and told the Governor about his discovery. The Governor had the man show him the severed head and at once convened an emergency meeting of the Elders. After an urgent discussion about the matter, they concluded that the time had come to dissolve the relationship between the Commoners and the Colonists. The missed community work assignments, odd behavior, and the lack of goodwill between the groups was one thing, but the hanging severed head was the last straw.

That evening a meeting was called between the Governor, the Elders and the Commoners. The Governor and the Elders decided to exclude the inhabitants of the Colony fearing that violence would break out with news of the outrage committed, although thanks to the town grapevine, everyone had already become aware of the severed head. At the meeting when asked about the severed head, the Leader said that the severed head was Commoner's business and of no concern to the general population of the Colony. That was not good enough for the Governor and the Elders who continued to push for an explanation.

The Leader, who by this point was as fed up with the Colonists and realizing that the end of their association was near, expressed his frustration plainly. He said that his congregants left England because they were tired of other people and the government constantly sticking their nose in their business. They came to the new world to be able to live as they pleased but that life here in the colonies was no better than life was in England. They put up with the Colonists because of the wilderness of the new world but they were losing patience with the constant interference by the Colony. They just wanted to live in peace and live with their ways and beliefs. As far as the severed head was concerned, that was Commoner's business, but he would explain anyway.

The head belonged to one of the new Colony converts. The Leader said that the man was caught reading a book, two nights previously. Reading a book other than the Bible would instill worldly knowledge and was therefore the ultimate sin. Knowledge interferes with simple living and unquestioning devotion to God's will. Any deviance from God's will, according to the Leader, would not be tolerated by the group and demanded swift and harsh punishment. He went on to say that he and his congregants felt that they were living among sinners because the Colonists read books other than the Bible, encouraged learning, and sent their children to school.

The more the Leader talked, the more agitated he and the Commoners became. They appeared on the brink of a frenzy. The Governor and his staff were getting nervous and sent one of the Elders to notify the militia to stand at the ready in case the Commoners went over the edge. Despite the consequences, the Governor and the Elders knew they had to cut ties. They told the Leader that relations between the two groups had progressed beyond repair and that he and the Commoners would have to leave the Colony as soon as possible. Although he knew it was coming, the Leader became enraged. He cursed the Governor, the Elder, and the Colonists as heathens and sinners. The Leader said they would leave in the morning but to beware, swearing revenge on the Colony for their wicked ways and promising that retaliation would be swift and harsh! With that dramatic warning, the Commoners stormed out of the meeting hall, their black cloaks flapping.

The next morning the Colonists found that the Commoners were gone, their crude huts abandoned. Some of the Colonists had tried to be charitable and helpful to the Commoners even though their peculiar ways and behavior had made them uneasy, however, the general feeling was that everyone was glad that the source of tension was gone. Besides, another ship was expected in the not-too-distant future. Everyone was sure that things would be fine with the new group of settlers. Life went on, and the Commoners were soon forgotten with more important matters to be focused on.

* * *

Six to eight months after the Commoners disappeared, the Colony found itself in an uproar again. During the night, several people from the Colony had gone missing. Everyone was ordered to assemble in the square for a headcount, only to find that five people had disappeared. Three Elders, the schoolteacher, and the pastor of the church were gone. An emergency meeting was held to discuss the situation. There were only two possibilities for the disappearance of the five people. One was the Native Americans who lived in the area. The townspeople did not think that the Native Americans were involved but they sent a Colony representative to check.

It was more likely that the Commoners were somehow responsible for the disappearance of the Elders, the schoolteacher, and the pastor because they had sworn revenge on the Colony. But where had the Commoners gone? No one knew. It would be a big problem finding them. The Native Americans were not responsible, however, they provided helpful information. Some tribe members had seen the Commoners heading north back around the time when the group was asked to leave the Colony. The Colonists trusted the Native Americans' intelligence. A group of the militia would be sent north to search for the Commoners, and hopefully rescue the missing people.

A through search was made of the surrounding lands north of the Colony but none of the missing were found. There was another settlement north of Plymouth, known as the Wessagusset Colony, which would later become Weymouth. The militia troop headed north to search and a week later arrived at what was left of the colony. The remaining Wessagussetians told the Plymouth militia that they were disbanding their group and intended to head south to Plymouth, hoping to integrate into their community.

This was due to trouble with the nearby Native Americans and a pack of strange settlers north of the Wessagusset Colony. When questioned, they told the Plymouth militia about their unnerving encounter with the peculiar settlers. The group's charismatic leader was also a literal mouthpiece, the only person who spoke, flanked by the ominous presence of the Commoner's members, staring out antagonistically toward the Wessagussetians like a flock of mute but terrifying crows.

The missing Wessagussetians included a schoolteacher, a pastor and one of their leaders. At that point, the militia knew the Commoners were responsible, and the militia captain shared that Plymouth's missing members had held similar community roles. The Plymouth militia made a deal with the remaining members of the Wessagussetians. They would escort them to the Plymouth Colony but first they wanted help in investigating the group they believed to be the Commoners. Everyone agreed and planned to leave first thing in the morning.

At first light, the fifteen members of the militia and twelve men from the Wessagusset Colony set out to find the Commoner's camp. They had no luck for two days but on the third they smelled smoke and crept in to investigate. The militia men saw replicas of the crudely built church and houses constructed by the Commoners in Plymouth. There was a ceremony going on in the middle of the camp. There, the militia men spied on the Leader, but it was unclear what was happening. With their loaded guns, they crept closer. What they then saw was a horrifying sight that would haunt them for years.

There was a tree in the middle of the camp. On that tree hung brains! Human brains twisted to and fro from the branches like ornaments on a perverted Christmas tree! Lying on the ground under the tree was the body of the Plymouth Colony schoolteacher. The Leader had sawn off the top of her head, and he stood over her body, with a handful of dripping bloody brains, about to drape them over a branch! It was too much for the militia and the Wessagutians to handle. As they rushed in, the Leader yelled for the Commoners to attack the sinners. The militia opened fire on the group killing most of them. The rest were either killed in hand-to-hand combat or surrendered. After the battle, the Leader and five captives were put in chains. The militia burned the tree decorated with brains, and they buried the schoolteacher before marching back to the Wessagusset Colony to pick up the remaining members. Then they all left for Plymouth Colony.

They arrived eight days later and met with the Governor. They told him the story and set a trial date three days forth. At the trial, as was the case before, only the Leader spoke. When asked why the brains were hung from the tree, he explained that that brains were containers of knowledge and knowledge was a great sin to the Commoners. He dangled the brains on the tree, just as he had hung the severed head at the Colony before, as a warning to the group to not acquire knowledge outside of what was needed to serve God's will. The leader had no other defense for his actions. The other members of the captured Commoners remained silent, never uttering a word in their defense. After a short deliberation, the court found the Leader and his five congregants guilty of murder and sentenced them to hang. The next morning, they were marched to the gallows on hilltop overlooking the Colony and hung by their necks. They were buried in unmarked graves. The Governor ordered the Colonists not to mention the Commoners again lest they be suspected of being sympathizers. The matter was considered put to rest.

But the incident was not wholly lost to the mists of time. Although the traumatic specifics of what happened there were mostly buried, the land remained marked by the incident. It became known as Braintree. Later when new settlers arrived and made the area a town, it was decided that it would be called Braintree to honor the poor colonists who died there.

CHAPTER 2
Raynham

The origin of the town name Raynham is rather humorous, except for the unfortunate loss of life. Raynham was established on April 2, 1731 but let us not get ahead of ourselves. The story starts many years prior to the establishment of the town. What was to become Raynham was originally part of East Taunton. Iron ore was discovered in the area in 1652. Settlers arrived shortly after that to start up an iron works. After people started arriving, it became an industrial district that housed a number of other industries that the region relied on for work and goods. Some of those included shoemaking, furniture companies, iron tools, sawmills, pottery, and tinsmiths and such. They even had a straw-hat factory down by the Two-Mile River.

The subject of our story is a meat processing plant. The plant was critical to the population of East Taunton. After all, this was way before refrigeration and meat had to be salted so it would last. The plant was started and owned by a man named Jacob Shurtleff. Mr. Shurtleff was an immigrant from Chipping Camden, England. Jacob's father was an essential player in the wool trade in Chipping Camden, as were most successful men in that area. The best wool in the world came from Chipping Camden and the towns surrounding that part of the country. Jacob's family was prosperous and lived a good life in the town, and Jacob benefited from his happy childhood. However, everyone must grow up, and that includes Jacob. The family's oldest son was expected to take over the business when he reached adulthood. This wasn't unique to the Shurtleff family; this was the way of all families in the area, especially wealthy families—it was an unquestioned convention.

However, for Jacob, spending the rest of his life running a sheep farm was not to his liking. It wasn't that Jacob did not like sheep, as he rather enjoyed playing with them as a boy in the fields. It's just that Jacob wanted more out of life than running a sheep farm. He reluctantly accepted his responsibilities and took over the farm because his father was in ill health.

After a few months, Jacob's father passed away, and Jacob saw his chance. Jacob's brother Isaiah had always been jealous that, as the oldest son, Jacob was expected to run the family farm. The brothers had a discussion, and Isaiah gladly took over the farm, which allowed Jacob to pursue other interests with his portion of the family's wealth. Shortly after leaving Chipping Camden, Jacob booked passage on the RMS William Smith and sailed out of Liverpool on May 14, 1728. Jacob arrived in Boston six weeks later. He began working at a meat packing house to save more money to start a business when the time was right. Jacob enjoyed his job and moved up the ranks very quickly. He thought he might want to start a meat processing facility, so he started exploring possible sites for it. He checked out about a dozen possibilities, but nothing seemed quite right.

One night at the local pub, Jacob talked to a man from a place called Taunton, about forty miles south of the city. He told Jacob about a site that he thought would be perfect for Jacob's proposed project. Jacob questioned the man thoroughly because travel in those days was not easy, and Jacob did not want to go on a wild goose chase. The man gave his assurances, so Jacob planned to scout the location. Jacob traveled to East Taunton, met his friend from the pub, and proceeded to see the site. Jacob liked it immediately and arranged to acquire the property the next day. The building was quickly completed, and Jacob set up his business. The Shurtleff Meat Processing and Packing Company was born.

The business was remarkably successful, and Jacob fit in well with the townspeople. Jacob was respected, ran a successful company, and even met a nice girl whose father owned the sawmill in town. He also got involved in local town politics. There was a movement to have part of East Taunton separate to become its own town. There was a lot of talking and arguing at many meetings, but the initiative was going to pass. The big sticking point of the succession was what the town would be called. Jonesville, Two Mile River, Clarksville: everyone had their own suggestions, but eventually, a name would need to be agreed upon. Jacob went about running his business and becoming more and more successful. He did beef and lamb processing, but his main product was pork. There were many pig farmers in the surrounding towns, and Jacob did quite well buying and processing pork. His smoked ham was very popular with local eating establishments and families.

One morning Jacob noticed some commotion outside his office window, and he went outside to see what was going on. A new building was being constructed next door to Jacob's plant. Wesson Smith owned it, and it was going to house a gunpowder plant and storage facility. Remember earlier I told you that the discovery of iron ore set the wheels in motion for the establishment of the town? During the ore extraction, explosives were used to help mine the ore. Shipping explosives was a costly and dangerous endeavor, so producing and storing them locally made sense. Jacob wished he had thought of creating an explosives company. Still, his business was doing so well, it employed ten men. And his products, especially his smoked ham, was hard to keep in stock, thanks to his loyal customers. He was doing so well that day and night shifts worked continuously around the clock at his plant. His one concern was the gunpowder company next door. Jacob had a bad feeling about it but could not put his finger on it.

As time passed, Jacob married the girl whose father owned the sawmill. They bought one of the finest houses around and got ready for his busiest season. Easter was only a few weeks away, and the Shurtleff Smoked Ham was so famous that restaurants and pubs from as far away as Boston and New York had placed orders. Jacob and his men were slammed trying to keep up with processing and packing smoked hams in time for Easter dinners all over the countryside. Hams were stacked to the ceiling, waiting to be shipped out. Jacob had his men work overtime the weekend before Easter to prepare for shipments that would commence on Monday morning. Jacob locked up the plant early Sunday afternoon and went home to get some rest for the busy week that would be coming up.

Business was also good next door at Wesson Smith's gunpowder plant. A big vein of iron ore had been discovered deep in the northeast part of town and the miners would need a large amount of gunpowder to extract it. Plenty of overtime was also being worked at the Smith plant in anticipation for Monday morning when the miners would start their pyrotechnics. Later Sunday afternoon, the work was completed at Wesson Smith's. The men gathered in the breakroom near the storage area for a pint to celebrate a job well done. Mr. Smith handed out cigars to his workers in appreciation for getting everything ready for the miners the next morning. Smith prepared to lock up, but a couple of the men wanted to have one for the road, so Smith's foreman assured Wesson that he would lock up. Mr. Smith, like Jacob, headed home for a good night's rest. Church was over for the day, and everyone was settling in for a tasty Sunday dinner when…

The noise was startling. A tremendous boom rattled through the town, shaking walls, and knocking pictures to the ground. Dishes and pans fell to the floor. Many houses close to the origin of the boom had shattered windows. Mr. Johnson's horse was so scared it died of a heart attack; dogs and cats hid under beds and tables. It was reported that people ten miles away had heard the noise and felt the vibrations. Everyone in town came running out of their houses to see what had happened. No one knew where the noise had come from.

Mrs. Jones, the shopkeeper's wife, was standing outside looking puzzled like everyone else when she felt something hit her head. Small, just a tap, but something. She looked over to James and Dorothy, her two children, and noticed something nestled in their hair. Mrs. Jones picked a piece of that something out of Dorothy's hair and examined it. "Strange," Mrs. Jones thought, "it looks like a piece of meat." She examined it, sniffed it, and discovered it was a knob of ham. Suddenly it was raining. But it wasn't water pouring from the sky; it was a hailstorm of ham! Everywhere you looked, pieces of pink ham were raining down from the sky. People ran back into their houses to avoid being hit by the ham falling from the sky. The more frugal townsfolk came back out with buckets to catch the ham, but most stayed inside until the ham shower was over.

The whole thing lasted about fifteen to twenty minutes, after which everyone came back out of their houses to clean up. Later, the Constable came around to ask questions and to figure out exactly what had happened. The investigation eventually led to the industrial part of town, where the Constable found, what he thought, was the source of the loud boom. Wesson Smith's gunpowder plant was no longer there; instead, only a giant smoking crater marked where it once stood. Some of the neighboring businesses also suffered moderate to heavy damages from the explosion. But none as much as Jacob Shurtleff's Meat Processing and Packing Plant. Jacob's building was also gone.

The following day the Constable rounded up all the principal parties for his investigation: Wesson Smith, Jacob Shurtleff, the other owners of the surrounding businesses, and Jacob and Wesson's employees. Wesson's foreman and two other men could not be located. After questioning all the people involved, especially Wesson Smith, the Constable deduced that after Wesson Smith had left his building, either his foreman or one of the other employees, (all presumed dead because no trace of them were ever found) had decided to smoke one of the cigars that Mr. Smith had given out to his employees. Somehow, the gunpowder storage was ignited by a tossed match or a burning cigar. Once ignited, the building blew up. Jacob's facility was only ten to twelve feet away from the gunpowder storage area of Mr. Smith's plant, and so the gigantic blast also destroyed Jacob's building. As previously noted, Jacob's plant was filled with smoked ham ready for delivery the next day. The force of the blast not only destroyed both buildings but also blew the ham far up into the sky resulting in the ham raining down on the town.

It took weeks to clean up the blast site and to collect all the ham that had rained down on the town. Neither Jacob Shurtleff nor Wesson Smith rebuilt their businesses. The townspeople blamed Mr. Wesson for the incident, and so he left the area. Jacob did not have the money or the will to rebuild, so he returned to the one thing he knew. Jacob Shurtleff moved to a neighboring town and established a sheep farm.

About six months after the big blast and the cleanup, the town leaders met again and proceeded with their separation from East Taunton. Oh, there was some arguing and disagreement on town boundaries and such, however, this time there was unanimous agreement for the name of their new town: Raynham.

CHAPTER 3

Mount Washington

Now, wait a minute, I thought this book was stories about how towns in *Massachusetts* got their names. Last time I checked, Mount Washington was in New Hampshire. That is true. Mount Washington is in New Hampshire, however, there is a town in Massachusetts named Mount Washington in the far southwest corner of the state and it is the third smallest town in Massachusetts. That could be why you have never heard of it. So, let's find out how it got its name.

The tale of how the town got its name has two principal players. One was Everett Taconic. Everett was a bold and boisterous man. The type who loved adventure and was not afraid to take chances. Win big or lose big. It did not matter to him. One of his big chances paid off and he acquired a great deal of the land that the town currently sits on. There was a range of mountains that ran through his land. He decided to name them the Taconic Mountain Range and he called the largest mountain Mount Everett. He liked to think that his mountains were of grand scale and that Everett Mountain was the tallest in the world. He did not really believe it but, it made him feel good to boast about it. He had a real Texas streak in him, and it was said that he was originally from that part of the country, but nobody knew for sure. But like I said, even though he was proud of his mountains, deep down he was a bit envious of the second character of our story, a Mister Manasseh Gorham.

Manasseh Gorham was a highly educated man from an old and respected family. He was born and spent his youth in Boston, graduated from Harvard, and taught there as a professor. He was prim and proper and had a high opinion of himself and a low opinion of most other people. But Mr. Gorham also had an adventurous side. Because he was from a wealthy family and had a trust fund, he organized a climbing party and headed north to New Hampshire to climb. He acquired the land that Waumbik Mountain stood on through some shrewd business dealings. Waumbik was the old Algonquian Indian name for the mountain. After getting it, he immediately changed the mountain's name from Waumbik to Mount Washington. He was a big admirer of George Washington, so he intended to honor the first President by naming the mountain after him. Since he owned the land and the mountain, Mr. Gorham could name it anything he wanted. So, he did the paperwork and made the necessary arrangements to have the mountain named Washington.

That was the easy part. Manasseh also wanted to set up a town on the mountain's land. He wanted the prestige of establishing and owning a town. He also planned on naming the town Mount Washington. But the state of New Hampshire would not let Manasseh incorporate his new town until certain requirements were met. Since the area around the mountain was sparsely populated, it would take some effort to set up a town. Manasseh went to work on it.

He started by recruiting, bribing, and coercing nearby people to settle on his land. He also worked on businesspeople he knew by arm twisting, intimidation, and, at last resort, calling in favors to find stores and services in his new town. Mr. Gorham was not well liked, and desperate measures were needed to start his town. Manasseh was making some progress, but he needed more people to settle in his new town to make it viable.

In the meantime, Everett Taconic had the same idea as Mr. Gorham. Everett wanted to create a town also. He loved his land and wanted to share it with people who would love it too. Mr. Taconic's problem was like Manasseh's: location. Everett's land was out of the way to say the least. He traveled the neighboring area trying to convince people to relocate. With some modest success, he also looked for businessmen to open shops in his still nameless new town. Everett's success was attributed to his likable personality as opposed to Manasseh's strongarm tactics, but both men still had a way to go before they could incorporate their towns. The two men were not the only ones with the same problem. Other wealthy men with land were also trying to establish their own towns with too few people and businesses. Fortunately, something was about to happen that would possibly be helpful to the two men.

Several prominent men in Boston came up with the idea of a re-settlement fair. It would be an informational hub for families and individuals interested in moving to one of the emerging towns in Massachusetts or neighboring states. Think of it like the college or vacation fairs we have nowadays when people come to a central location to learn more about the offerings outside the region. Instead of men like Everett and Manasseh traveling the countryside looking for new settlers, the settlers would all come to one place to learn what was available. It sounded like a good idea, and it was! The fair was held in Boston, well attended by people looking for a new start and businessmen looking for good opportunities.

It was a successful day for both Everett and Manasseh. Both men recruited many people and businessmen to move to their respective locations. However, their styles were as different as night and day. Everett Taconic was honest and forthcoming about the realities of moving to his new town. He didn't sugarcoat the challenges, and prospective buyers appreciated Everett's honesty. Manasseh took a different route. He embellished the situation and told a few fibs about what people could expect if they moved to his town. But Manasseh was able to railroad enough people to commit, making his day worthwhile.

That evening there was a celebration for the men who ran the settlement fair. All the entrepreneurs gathered for drinks to discuss the day's activities before dinner. It was during cocktail hour that Mr. Taconic was introduced to Mr. Gorham. Everett shook Manasseh's hand in his usual jovial way. After observing him before they were introduced, Manasseh took an instant dislike of Everett. He thought Everett was a country bumpkin, a big buffoon not remotely on the same level as himself. He made his feelings known to the group of men sharing drinks. Subtly, of course, but still unflattering to Mr. Taconic. Everett was displeased by the remarks but decided not to make a big deal about it. He thought Mr. Gorham was a jerk, but figured he would not be seeing him again, and he'd let it slide.

As luck would have it, Everett and Manasseh were seated at the same table for dinner. It was a fancy dinner with multiple courses allowing Manasseh plenty of opportunity to continue his harassment of Everett. Manasseh was subtle about it. He referenced his dislike of southerners and people who lacked proper refinement. He bragged about his fine university education and the best tailor to custom make one's clothing. This was all indirectly intended at Mr. Taconic.

Now granted, Everett knew that he didn't have the schooling, education, or social etiquette of Mr. Gorman. He also thought that Manasseh was lucky that he didn't have a short temper, but Everett wasn't as dumb as Manasseh thought. By their facial expressions and rolling eyeballs, Everett could tell that the other ten men at the table were thinking the same thing Everett was thinking, that Mr. Manasseh Gorham was a world-class jerk! So again, Everett let it slide off his back, again assuming that he wouldn't be seeing Manasseh again when dinner was over.

One of the men suggested a poker game after the party finished their dessert and coffee. We all know what Everett's answer was. Remember what I said about Everett at the beginning of the story, he wasn't afraid to take chances and win big or lose big? So obviously his answer was yes. Besides, despite Mr. Gorham's needling characterizations, Everett was quite wealthy. The men retired to a smaller room for drinks, cigars, and some poker.

During the game, the men discussed plans and locations of their potential towns. Mr. Gorham spoke of his ownership of the highest mountain in the northeast, his grandiose schemes, and how his town would be named after the mountain. Mount Washington would be the name of the biggest mountain and the biggest town in New Hampshire. When it was Everett's turn to talk about his town, Manasseh wasted no time tearing into Everett once again.

Fortified with a few too many drinks, Manasseh openly made fun of the location of Everett's land. He wondered why anyone on earth would want to live in such a godforsaken place, in the middle of nowhere. He cast aspersions that Everett had the financial capital or the smarts to make it happen. And red-faced, he peppered his alcoholic tirade with offensive jokes about "Mount Everett" calling it nothing but an overgrown hill!

At that point, Everett wanted nothing more than to overturn the table and punch Mr. Gorham in his big, blabbering mouth. It was all he could do to maintain his temper after the steady stream of abuse he had endured over the evening. Earlier in the evening he could ignore it, especially knowing how the other men at the table felt about Mr. Gorham. But Manasseh's remarks during the game were too much to take. The other men were watching Everett to see what he would do. Everett mulled over how he would deal with Mr. Gorham. Then the next hand was dealt. When Everett looked at his cards, he had an answer.

The gameplay continued, and bets and raises were made in quick succession. It appeared that many players had potentially good hands. The dealer asked the players how many cards they wanted,

"I'll take two."

"I'll take three."

"I'll take one."

The dealer asked Manasseh how many cards he wanted, and he confidently shook his head no. The dealer then turned to Everett and asked the same question. Everett smiled graciously and said, "I'll play these." Once again, bets were made, raises were made, and the other players, one by one, dropped out. Only Mr. Gorham and Mr. Taconic remained in the game, a veritable call and response of betting. Manasseh never wanted to win a hand in poker more than this one.

"How dare this country bumpkin, this southerner, think he can beat me. I went to Harvard," thought Manasseh obsessively between each bet. "I'm a rich gentleman from Boston, and I own the highest, biggest mountain around," Manasseh reminded himself.

Every time Everett reraised him, he could not call despite the increasingly high stack of bills on the table. Manasseh's taunting was not enough; he wanted to teach Everett a proper lesson and put him in his bottom-dwelling place. Once again, Manasseh reraised him. A big reraise. An enormous reraise. A reraise that could scuttle his plans to build his town around Mount Washington. Manasseh thought there was no way Everett could call, let alone reraise him. A crowd had gathered around the poker table, and the other players were shocked by the amount of money on the table. Everett looked at the reraise, paused, and looked at his cards and the dwindling supply of chips while pondering his next move.

Manasseh observed Everett's hesitation and assessing the chips as a sign that his position was weak. If Everett had a good hand, he would bet without hesitation. Everett looked at his cards and chips several times then said, "reraise." Everett pushed the rest of his chips into the pile and said, "And my land."

Mr. Gorham almost fell off his chair. He didn't know what to do for a moment. The other players and spectators just stared at Manasseh, waiting to see his response. Manasseh looked at his cards. Full house, aces over kings. Not the best poker hand, but as good could be hoped for. "Could he have a better hand than mine?" puzzled Manasseh. "Is he bluffing? Doesn't he know any better? Could this simpleton beat me?" Manasseh's mind was churning. While he was in too deep to fold, he couldn't risk his land and mountain on it.

Manasseh briefly considered the situation and said, "It's not proper to bet property in a game when the stakes are for money." Manasseh believed that he figured out a way to stay in the hand and not lose everything in the unlikely event that Everett had a better hand. Everett didn't want Manasseh to wriggle out of the bet. Everett knew that money wasn't the motivation behind Manasseh's statement; Manasseh did not want to lose his land. Everett wanted nothing more than to punish Manasseh after the night of abuse he endured from him. But he knew that Mr. Gorham would not call the bet if he insisted that Manasseh call the bet. For Everett, the money was irrelevant. But how to stick it Mr. Gorham? Then it came to him.

"I'll tell you what Mr. Gorham" Everett said, "I'll let my bet stand. The land and the money. All you must do is match the money and bet the name of your town against my land."

Manasseh could not believe it! "How dumb could this southern bumpkin be! He is betting his land against a name. I'll probably win the hand anyway," he thought. How could he not call the hand? Before Manasseh could say, "I call," Everett said, "We need to make this bet legal." Everett asked if there were any lawyers in attendance. There were, and Everett had the lawyer quickly draw up a document that spelled out the legal responsibilities over the outcome of the bet. The document stated if Everett lost the bet, Manasseh would own Everett's land in Massachusetts. If Manasseh lost the bet, he could never use the name Mount Washington for his town. With a flourish, Everett signed the document. He put the paper on top of the chips on the table and said, "Do you call?"

Knowing all Everett's land and money were on the table, Manasseh quickly called and signed the document. A hush went over the room. Manasseh laughed as he turned over his cards. "Full house, aces over kings," he said. He looked at Everett's expressionless face and said, "Maybe I'll open a town for lowlifes in Massachusetts," as he reached for the document and chips.

"Don't you want to see my cards?" said Everett.

"Does it matter?" Manasseh laughingly remarked.

"I think so," said Everett. Everett turned over his cards one by one, a two followed by a three followed by a four followed by a five followed by a six. All diamonds. A straight flush. Manasseh's mood quickly changed from triumphant to dour. "Thank you, Mr. Gorham," said Everett, "It was a pleasure playing cards with you." Then Everett let out a big, booming laugh. The other players and spectators around the table shared in the laughter and heartily congratulated Everett. Mr. Gorham slunk out of the hall.

Mr. Gorham eventually started his town in New Hampshire and named it after himself, "Gorham." Everett built his town in Massachusetts, gleefully calling it "Mount Washington." For Everett, knowing that every time Manasseh Gorham looked at a map of Massachusetts, he would remember the time that southern bumpkin beat him in a game of poker was priceless!

CHAPTER 4
Cheshire

Cheshire is a small town of about 3,200 near Pittsfield in the Berkshires. Cheshire was first settled in around 1766 and officially incorporated in 1793. It is named after the county of Cheshire in England. Now, that is the official version of how the town got its name. But we know better, don't we?

The town was first settled by Baptists from Rhode Island. The first settlers in the region were not from the established Puritan Church. The early colonists were instead, mostly descendants of those who had followed Roger Williams to Rhode Island to practice freely. These new settlers called their new settlement Stafford after one of the emigration leaders. The town had forges and sawmills, grist mills and tanneries, and in 1812, the Cheshire Crown Glass Company opened, as did a triphammer operation. The town also had the first factory in western Massachusetts to manufacture cotton-making machinery. That's all well and good, however this is 1766 and the main industry was dairy farming and cheese making.

Stafford and its residents were strongly partisan in the election battles of the country's early days. The Adams-Jefferson election of 1800 was hard fought, and Stafford was the only Berkshire town that favored Jefferson. When their candidate won the election, the town searched for a way to show their support and pay tribute to their new president. Because Stafford specialized in dairying and making cheese, they decided to send the president a gift of Stafford cheese. John Cheshire was the biggest, most popular and, by unanimous consent, the maker of the best cheese in town. John had been a dairy farmer back in Rhode Island and decided to join the group headed to Massachusetts. Everyone knew and liked John and his wife Mary. Maybe even more popular was John's cat, and an unusual cat it was. John's cat was always smiling, with a big grin that showed almost all its teeth. No one knew why the cat was always smiling. Perhaps it was born like that , but most people surmised that it was because John made the best cheese and his cat loved to eat it. The cat had a name, but everybody just called it Cheshire. Even John and Mary started to call it Cheshire.

John went to work and created quite the cheese for the new president. The cheese was 4 feet in diameter, 18 inches thick, and weighed 1,235 pounds. It was moved on a sled drawn by six horses when it was shipped off to Washington, D.C., where it drew a personal letter of thanks from President Jefferson. John and the residents of Stafford were all very proud of the recognition from President Jefferson. So proud that a proposal to change the town's name from Stafford to Cheshire was made at a community meeting. The vote was unanimous in naming the town Cheshire. For a while, John's cat, Cheshire was on even on the official town seal. One of the two monuments in Cheshire commemorates the cheese; the other memorializes the town's founders.

On a side note, around the time this was happening, a couple of travelers from England were visiting the town. A Mr. Carroll and his young son Lewis who later in life wrote a famous book that had a grinning cat. Coincidence? Maybe. I'll let you figure that one out.

CHAPTER 5
Brockton

So, the city that is now Brockton, Massachusetts was once called North Bridgewater. Bridgewater was originally part of Duxbury back in the 1600's. Then part of it became Pembroke and a court decreed this, and the Governor proclaimed that, and so on. That's a whole different story. We're gonna focus on the 1800's when the name change happened. Now in the 1830s we had four separate towns in the area. Bridgewater, East Bridgewater, West Bridgewater, and North Bridgewater. Back in those days, most of the land in these towns was farmland. The four towns were sparsely populated with small town centers. In each of the towns, there were one or two men who owned most of the land in the town. That was the case in North Bridgewater.

Robert Thurston was that man in North Bridgewater. Robert was a wealthy farmer who owned almost all of North Bridgewater. The Thurston name had a long and storied history in the area. He married his high school sweetheart and had three daughters and a son. Robert's son Richard owned much of West Bridgewater. Richard had a huge dairy farm. Some of the locals called him "Big Barn Smell," although not to his face. You see Dick, what he liked to be called, was a big stocky man. He was tough and could fight like no one in the area. Don't get me wrong, Dick was a nice guy, but his punch was like a block of granite and you did not want to be on the other end of that!

Wealthy people tend to have time to pursue other activities because they hire other people to do the work. This was the case for Robert Thurston and his son Richard. Like I said before, Dick was a tough man and liked to take part in boxing matches, managed by his father, who set up the matches and handled the details. These matches would be for money. Usually, the winner would get the purse but sometimes it would be split, 70-30 or something similar. However, the real money was made by betting on the matches. Dick and his father could usually make ten times the amount of the purses by betting on the fights, and Dick never lost. The two of them would travel throughout New England and down to New York and New Jersey for fights. They were well known in the fight circles. So well-known that, due to their success, fights were becoming few and far between.

Another name that was being heard around boxing circles was Isaac Brock. Not much was known about him. He did most of his fighting in the Midwest. Like Dick, Isaac didn't like to be called by his first name. His nickname was Rocky. It was said that Rocky's punch was like being hit with a ton of bricks. People who had seen some of his matches said that just before he hit you with the knockout punch he would yell "Here comes the ton!" Rocky had an unblemished fight record. 26-0. Consequently, he was having a hard time finding opponents. No one wanted to fight him. Rocky and his manager talked about it and decided that they would head east where fighters were less likely to have heard of him. Besides, it was known that most of the better boxers fought in the northeast area of the US.

So, Rocky and his manager got on a train and headed for New York. They spent a year in New York and had eleven fights, averaging almost one a month. Now remember, this was the mid 1800s and there were no boxing commissions to regulate the number of fights that a boxer could have within a certain time period. They were all early KOs for Rocky. The longest match went three rounds, so there wasn't much of a toll on his body. Rocky was making good money, but word was getting out about him and, with a few exceptions, his manager was starting to find it hard to line up fights. What had happened back in the Midwest was starting to happen in New York. Like I explained before, Rocky was so good that very few fighters wanted to climb in the ring with him and get their head beat in for hopefully 30% of the purse, and no hope for betting money because they knew they would lose. This also affected Rocky. Even getting 100% of the purse, there was no big money to be made betting because no one would bet against him. Rocky didn't realize it, but his problem was he was born too early. Had he been born 100 years later; he could have made a fortune. With boxing commissions, world championships, endorsements and commercials and movies, he'd be rolling in the money. However, that was all a moot point because you can't miss what you don't know. Rocky would lie awake at night thinking how he could make a big score boxing. A real big score! He could not know it at the time lying there in his bed but, that big score was coming soon.

A good friend of Robert Thurston had been in New York and went to a couple of Rocky's fights. When he got back, he told Robert, "This kid is a hell of a fighter!" He raved to him about the matches he saw.

"He may be good, but he couldn't beat my boy Dick," Robert boasted. "Don't be too sure" his friend said, "I'd have a hard time deciding who to put my money on." This irked Robert. He did not like people thinking there was someone out there that was better than his son. After all, Robert thought, Dick had fought all over New England, New York, and New Jersey and had never lost a match. He knew his friend would blab all over the Bridgewater area about this Rocky character and cast doubt on Dick being the best fighter around. The more Robert thought about this, the madder he got. Robert knew what he would have to do. He would travel to the telegraph office in the morning.

Robert met with his son the next day. Dick had told his father that he was getting older and was thinking about devoting his time to his dairy business. He wasn't too keen on getting into the ring again. He and Robert went back and forth on this. Robert finally convinced Dick that this would be his last fight and they would bet big and make one more big score before they both retired from the fight game and concentrated on their businesses. Dick reluctantly agreed to fight Rocky. Robert went to the telegraph office and sent a message to Rocky's manager , John Smythe, proposing a fight between his fighter and Dick. John Smythe was reluctant. He didn't want to travel all the way to Massachusetts because they were fighting in Florida for the foreseeable future. Robert responded that he meant to make this a huge score fight with a sizable purse and some big bets on the side. John Smythe told Robert that he would check with his fighter and get back to him.

Rocky was excited about the proposal. He wanted to make a big score. A tremendous score. To Rocky this looked like the fight he had been waiting for. John Smythe wired Robert Thurston and accepted the fight contingent upon negotiations on purse size and "other things." They would travel to North Bridgewater to meet after Rocky's fight next week.

Rocky and John arrived in North Bridgewater as scheduled. John felt like they were in the middle of nowhere but Rocky liked the area. It was refreshing to be out in the country after spending so much time in cities. They met at Robert Thurston's house. After introductions they had a nice dinner. Drinks and cigars after led up to the negotiations. First, they discussed the purse. They decided to hold the fight in Boston. There, they could hold it in a large venue, which would increase the size of the purse. It was decided that the purse would be split 60-40. A conservative split, Robert thought, but maybe they had doubts about beating Dick and would want to walk away with something. Then came the interesting part, the private bets. Large sums of money were discussed. During the discussions, Rocky was assessing his opponent. He knew that Dick had never lost a fight. "A big tough man for sure," thought Rocky but he didn't see the fire in Dick's eyes. Rocky knew at that moment he would win this fight. He also knew by listening to the conversation that Robert was totally convinced that his son would win. "This is the big score," thought Rocky.

Rocky joined into the conversation and said that he didn't think this fight would be beneficial to him. He didn't think that Dick would make a worthy opponent and he thought he could beat Dick handily. He said he doubted that Robert would have the money to back up the bets. John Smythe was a bit miffed by Rocky's comments, but he knew Rocky had a motive. Robert was livid over Rocky's comments. He was so enraged that he was not thinking straight. Rocky had him right where he wanted him, and he made a proposal. "I'll tell you what Mr. Thurston, I'll fight your boy, but these are the conditions. 100% of the purse goes to the winner. Also, my manager and I will put up one million dollars and you put up your land. Winner takes all." Dick jumped up and said, "Dad no! You can't make that bet." But Robert was too angry and quickly agreed to the bout. Contracts were signed and Rocky and his John Smythe bid them "Good night." The match would be held in three weeks' time.

After they left the manager said to Rocky, "I hope you know what you're doing. We don't have anywhere near a million dollars to pay that bet if you lose. We'll end up in jail!" Rocky just smiled at him and said, "Don't worry, I got this one. This will be the big score we have been waiting for. I'll have money and immortality after this fight. And you get ten percent of it," laughed Rocky. "Let's get some sleep. I got lots of training starting tomorrow."

At last, it was fight night and Rocky felt great. There was a big crowd who had paid to see the fight so that meant a larger purse. The fighters were announced, and the bell rang. The fighters were feeling each other out for the first few rounds. By the fourth round, massive fists were flying and connecting with loud thumps. Sitting in the corner after the eighth round, Rocky was thinking that his opponent was tougher than he figured, but he was confident. He still had seven more rounds to put Dick Thurston on the deck. By the twelfth round Rocky knew that if he was careful, he'd put Dick down by the fourteenth. Sure enough, in the fourteenth round, Rocky had pummeled his opponent with a couple of hard rights and lefts. He could see in Dick's eyes that the next big punch would end it. Rocky saw his opening and yelled "Here comes the ton!" Rocky had hit Dick square on the jaw with a haymaker. The referee counted to ten and it was over. Rocky had won the fight. Celebrations went late into the night. Rocky was now a landowner and 50,000 dollars richer from the purse plus a "few dollars more" made on side bets. Rocky had his big score!

After Rocky recouped from the fight, he and his manager went to see a land lawyer to finalize the contract details that he and Robert had signed. Rocky wanted to change the name of North Bridgewater. He had his money, now he wanted his immortality. Rocky wanted to change the name of his newly won town to "Brock". His manager suggested to Rocky that the name sounded a little short and he should combine his name and his signature fight call and name his new town Brock-ton . Rocky liked the idea and so Brockton it became.

Rocky enjoyed living in Brockton for a while but he missed the big city. He contacted and set up a meeting with Robert Thurston. Rocky offered to sell the land he won in the fight back to Robert. Robert had been paying rent on his farm to Rocky and jumped at the chance. Rocky received a very nice sum of money for the land and kept a few acres for himself that he would visit from time to time. The only provision that Rocky wanted in the sales contract was that the name Brockton could never be changed. Although another Rocky would come along years later and make Brockton famous, the first Rocky is how Brockton got its name.

CHAPTER 6
Wellfleet

Arrrrrrgh, pull up a chair ya scurvy dog and let me tell you a tale of pirates and the sea. The town of Wellfleet sits halfway up on the outer arm of Cape Cod. The area that Wellfleet now stands was once called Billingsgate, originally part of Eastham. The ocean plays crucial role in the town's economy. In the early 1700s, Billingsgate was a center for fishing, shell fishing, and whaling. It was the lifeblood of the residents, and they made a good living from the sea. Aside from some formidable storms that passed through, especially in the winter, there were not many barriers to earning a reliable income.

Billingsgate was also known for something besides fishing. Black Sam Bellamy was a well-known pirate. The early 1700s were the glory days for pirates and Black Sam was one of the most successful of them. Most pirates spent their time in the Caribbean and the American South, but Black Sam was one of the few that ventured further north. One compelling reason he would sail to the township was that Black Sam was smitten with a woman he had met on one of his voyages to Billingsgate. On one of his earlier trips to the area, he made the acquaintance of a one Miss Michelle Hallett Michelle was a pretty woman of about twenty-five, a daughter of one of the fishing families of Billingsgate. Everyone knew Michelle by the big pink fluffy hat she always wore. Most of the people in town called her Fluff because of her hat and that hat is what first got Black Sam's attention.

Black Sam would frequent The Squire Inn, a local tavern in Billingsgate. Michelle worked at the tavern, and that is where Sam first encountered her. Black Sam, like most pirates, had a woman in every port, but there was something especially intriguing about Fluff. Sam tried to get to know Fluff better, but she was uninterested in Sam although he was a famous pirate. After sailing to Billingsgate, Black Sam would go to the tavern to see Fluff, but she refused to flirt, and only cared to do her job serving him food and ale. This seemed to be the case during all of Sam's visits. Black Sam never plundered the waters around Billingsgate, and the townspeople believed it was because of his feelings for Michelle. The locals urged Fluff to cozy up to Sam to keep him from doing anything bad to them, reminding her how wealthy he was. But she was true to her principles and refused to change her mind. Fluff didn't like Sam because she thought he had no virtues, that he was simply a bad character. After many visits, Sam lost patience with Fluff's cool demeanor and told some of his shipmates that things would be different the next time they came to Billingsgate.

He departed, and unknown to Black Sam, Fluff was getting off her shift at the same time and followed him out of the tavern. Out on the street a sailor was abusing a dog. The dog looked pretty beaten up and the man continued to yell at and hit the dog. Black Sam, who had his faults, was nevertheless an animal lover. He ran up to the man and punched him square in the face. The man fell to the ground. Sam picked him up and yelled, "How dare you hit a defenseless dog!" Sam punched him several times and then tossed him into the mud. "If I catch you hitting an animal again, I'll break your legs" Sam said. Sam gently picked up the dog and comforted him.

Fluff stood wide-eyed watching the events unfold. She suddenly saw Black Sam differently. Fluff was an animal lover and maybe she had been wrong about Black Sam. Fluff ran up to Sam and began patting the dog. "That was wonderful Sam," she said, "the way you helped this poor dog." Their eyes met and Sam knew that things had changed. From that point on, Black Sam and Fluff became a couple. Black Sam would come back to Billingsgate as often as possible to visit with Fluff. Sam and Fluff were happy, and the townspeople were relived. Rumors around town were that Black Sam asked Fluff to marry him, and sure enough, these rumors were true. Fluff accepted Sam's proposal and the wedding was scheduled for Sam's return from his latest voyage.

After some successful "encounters" in Tortola, Black Sam and his crew headed back to Billingsgate for the wedding. Just as they got to Cape Cod, a fearsome storm hit. Black Sam pressed on and got to Billingsgate, five hundred feet from shore, when the ship capsized drowning all but two sailors aboard. When the storm passed, the townspeople searched the coastline and found the body of Black Sam. Fluff was terribly upset. The town had a funeral for Black Sam and any sailors they could find. Time passed, and life went on in the town. But things were about to get difficult for the residents of Billingsgate. Very difficult.

Black Sam was one of the most prominent pirates of his time. All the pirates knew that Cape Cod, especially Billingsgate, was Sam's territory, and other pirates were unwilling to trespass. However, Black Sam had died, and Cape Cod became fair game for other pirates. Things were getting hot in the Caribbean with the British Navy patrolling the waters, so pirates were looking for other places to plunder.

A few months after Black Sam's death, pirates began showing up off the coast of Cape Cod, and anyone on a boat was vulnerable. Fishing boats, whalers, and especially merchant ships were in danger of attack. When the pirates couldn't find any ships to attack, they would come ashore and terrorize the towns. Billingsgate was no exception. The pirates would get drunk and raise hell. They took what they wanted from stores, and burned them down if they couldn't find what they wanted. They took women they found attractive and fought men who looked at them the wrong way. The pirates were also very curious about Fluff. Some townspeople hid Fluff from the pirates and told them that she had left the town after Black Sam's death. Sometimes the pirates believed it, sometimes they didn't and ripped people's houses apart looking for her. Fortunately for Fluff, she hadn't been found up to now. Things had become awful for the residents of Billingsgate and the other towns on Cape Cod. Something had to be done, and someone needed to stop the pirates.

That person was Josh Wells. Josh was a captain of one of the whaling ships that ran out of Nantucket. Josh was a rugged and righteous man and wanted to take charge. He was fortunate that his ship hadn't been attacked by the pirates, but he knew it was just a matter of time. Josh's idea was to organize all the fishermen and whalers and form a fleet of ships. The fleet would fight and drive the pirates out of Cape Cod waters. Josh and the other ship captains pledged their boats to battle the pirates. Each captain secured as many cannons, guns, and armaments as possible. As scheduled, they met in the most centralized location, Billingsgate, to plan the attacks on the pirates.

Josh came to Billingsgate a couple of days before the meeting to finalize plans before all the other ship captains came for the meeting. Josh wanted to talk to Fluff and get any information on Black Sam that might be helpful. Fluff met Josh at the Squire Inn. Fluff and Josh talked for hours. Some conversations were about Black Sam, but most of it was general chit-chat arising from a spark between the two. Josh met with Fluff over the next few days while waiting for the big meeting with other captains. Josh's growing feelings for Fluff intensified his determination to deal with the pirates.

The other ship captains arrived and discussed how to get rid of the pirates. They chose Josh Wells as the head of the fleet. Inventory of armaments and ammunition was taken, and the strength of each ship was assessed. Josh's plan was to split the fleet into two groups. Most of the plundering by the pirates was done on the bayside where the harbors were. Remember, this was before the Cape Cod Canal so the only way into the bay was from the open ocean. One group of the ships would go after the pirates on the ocean side before they got to Cape Cod Bay. The pirates would be outnumbered so they would be corralled into the bay. The second group, already in the bay, would attack. The pirates would be outnumbered and caught with attackers on both sides. All the ship captains agreed on the plan and put it into action the following morning.

Josh's plan worked perfectly. Every pirate ship sailing by was easily defeated. Within six months, word had got out in the pirate community about the Josh Wells' fleet and the pirates finally stopped coming to Cape Cod. Josh continued to see Fluff, and he eventually moved to Billingsgate from Nantucket when he married her.

In 1763, after thirty years of petitioning for town status, the commonwealth granted Billingsgate the right to become a town. The town fathers held a public meeting. During the meeting, changing the name of Billingsgate was brought up. The townspeople wanted a new name now that they were now going to be separated from Eastham. Several names were suggested before seventy-one-year-old Fluff Wells walked to the front of the meeting hall. Everyone knew and respected Fluff and the room went silent as they waited for her to speak.

Fluff said, "Many years ago, our town was nearly destroyed by pirates. If it hadn't been for my dear departed husband, we would not be sitting here now discussing a new name for our beloved town. Josh Wells' fleet of ships saved us and our town from the pirates, and I think we should call our new town Wellsfleet. We're a small town with a big heart and my heart tells me, that would be the thing to do. Thank you." With that, Fluff returned to her seat. The crowd stood and applauded her suggestion. The town fathers agreed and decided to change the town's name to Wellsfleet. But wait a minute. What happened to the s in Wellsfleet? A clerical error in the submission papers in Boston dropped the "s". The town fathers tried to correct it, but, well, you know how the government is.

CHAPTER 7
Florida

Florida is tiny town located in the Berkshires. Most of what is now Florida was originally a grant to the town of Bernardston, Massachusetts, made sometime before 1771. The first settler, Dr. Daniel Nelson, arrived around 1783. In 1805 the town was incorporated. Influential men in the area discussed the details and name of the new town. They met at the meetinghouse to start the work on incorporation. The meeting began at eight in the morning. Despite the warm July day, the men showed up in their finest clothing to impress. Suits, their best shirts, top hats, shined shoes, walking sticks, the whole nine yards. Every man wanted to look his best to influence the others.

The morning business went quick with very little discussion or debate. All the items needed for incorporation were finished before noon. The only thing left was to come up with a suitable name for the new town. Now if you're thinking everything was going too smoothly, you are right. Even though the men mostly agreed on the articles, when it came time to name the town, each person had their own idea. One man wanted West Bernardston, another wanted Nelsonville, and few wished the glory of naming the town after themselves. The discussion of the naming became heated. Perhaps influencing the heated conversation was the fact that the temperature inside the building was rising by the hour.

It was a particularly humid day even for July. As time went on, all of those articles of finery the men were wearing, were discarded, one by one. Top hats were laid on the table, suitcoats hung on chairs, ties were irritably loosened or flung off, sleeves rolled up, inch by inch. No one was concerned about impressing the others as the temperature inside the building reached the high nineties. The debate raged on for hours with no consensus on a name for the town. Someone suggested that maybe the meeting could be continued outside where it might be cooler than in the building. They could agree on that, and the men adjourned to the yard behind the meetinghouse.

Although there was fresher air outside, it was still hot! Shoes and socks were discarded, and bare feet dug into the grass. The dispute on the name continued but they still were nowhere near a consensus. Suddenly, the men began removing their shirts, trying to cool off. They continued talking and in the merciless heat, one by one and still talking, many of the men ditched their undershirts and some removed their pants and sat on the ground in their shorts. The endless arguing went back and forth for the best town name. At some point, they decided to take a break and the men reclined on the lawn, taking a breather, closing their eyes, and enjoying the feeling of the grass. Just then, a group of women walked by. One of the women who used to live down south looked at the men lying in the grass in their underwear and remarked, "You men look like you're living in Florida." The other women laughed and kept walking on their way. The men all sat up and looked at each other. They smiled, and one said, "I think we have a name for our town."

CHAPTER 8

Franklin, Wrentham, and Sheldonville

T his is the tale of how two towns and a neighborhood between those town s got their names. We will start with Franklin, named after Benton Franklin, a distinguished and wealthy man who owned most of the land that the town stood on. The town was originally named Exeter, but the town fathers voted to change the name to Franklin after Benton donated a grand bell for the church steeple. The church's belfry was empty for years and was a source of embarrassment for the pastor of the church and the town. Benton was not much of a churchgoing man, but he was kindly and generous and felt bad for the townspeople. Big brass bells were costly, but Benton felt the church really needed it, and he was deeply appreciative when they changed the town's name in his honor. Benton had done a lot for Franklin previously, but the bell donation especially touched the townspeople's hearts. However, Benton Franklin is not the focus of our story, his son William Franklin is.

William Franklin was Benton's only child and had a personality totally opposite of his father. When William was a child, he was constantly embroiled in trouble. As kind and caring as his father was, William was self-centered and had no compassion for anyone but himself. He was a clever person and the type to take advantage of you when you think he is doing you a favor. Unfortunately, Benton was blind to his son's character, so no corrections to William's behavior ever stuck despite the complaints from his teachers and other people.

After graduating from school, William left the area to attend collage for business. With his diploma in hand William looked to make his mark in the world when his father fell sick. Reluctantly William returned home to care for his father. Still, all he could think about was what he could do with the inheritance he would receive. You see, Benton was a widower and had no other children, so William was planning to inherit a good deal of money and land. Not much more than a week passed since William returned, when Benton died. After the funeral and the reading of the will, William took possession of the house, which was the grandest in town, and began planning his future.

While William knew that he wanted to start a new business, he was not sure what kind. He did not have any specific knowledge of any industry , but he was very self-confident. So, he pondered the subject, thinking about what he enjoyed doing throughout his young life. He thought about his grandfather, who was a sea captain. When he was in port in either Boston or New Bedford, his grandfather would come and call upon William's parent's when William was a child. William loved listening to his grandfather's tales of the sea and sometimes even visited his ship docked in the port. If the weather were good, his grandfather would even take William out on the water for an overnight trip, as long as William behaved himself. William's grandfather could see his grandson's flawed character, unlike Benton and his daughter. He did his best in the limited time he spent with William to straighten him out, and he was often the only one who could get through to William. Although William loved his grandfather and was thrilled to go on his grandfather's sailing ship, he knew he did not want to be a ship captain. He studied business in college and wanted to use his knowledge to start a new business. Unfortunately, the only opportunity on his newly acquired land was farming. There were farms for miles as far as the eye could see, and although he liked the rent payments he received from the farmers, he left because he had no interest in farming. William spent some time reflecting, and then it suddenly came to him.

"I loved my grandfather's ship, but I don't want to be a sea captain," considered William, "So why don't I build ships instead! That's it," he thought. "I've got the land, and I've got the money." The strange thing about his plan was that he wasn't near the water. Most boatbuilding was done at the docks on the oceanfront, not miles inland. But he believed that would make his boats unique. Nautical types who were in the market to purchase a ship would undoubtedly be curious to learn about his inland shipyard putting him first in their minds. William began to plan the work to start his business.

With the money he had inherited, he could start the boatbuilding business, and he had the farmers' land rent payments for a steady income during the buildup for his business. He knew that the unusual location would only get him so far, so he had to build the best quality boats. "So far, so good," he thought, "Here is where the plan gets sticky." He would need the best shipwrights to build the best boats, which would be expensive. He would have to recruit them from the docks in Boston and elsewhere and convince them to move inland to work for him. And he would have to pay them well. Very well. Even if he could get the workers to work for him, he wondered where they would live, because Franklin was all farmland, and any suitable housing was far away. The workers would also probably want to bring their families to their new place of employment, so building dormitories was not a solution.

Also, there would be additional logistics and expenses of transporting the newly built boats to the harbor many miles away. William had some problems to work out if he wanted to start his boatbuilding business in Franklin. The wheels spun in his head and suddenly an idea emerged on how he could pay his workers top dollar yet barely lose any money on their wages. "It's brilliant!" he exclaimed aloud. He went to work directly on implementing his plan.

William first negotiated with the farmers who owned large, unused barns—the perfect space to build large ships, because it would be cheaper than building new structures. William had the upper hand because he owned the land and made deals they couldn't refuse. Besides, he would need the money for the most ingenious part of his plan. William owned the land in the southeastern part of Franklin, where he would build housing for the workers he needed. It was there that he built rows of connected houses. Kitchen, living room, and bath on the first floor with two bedrooms on the second floor. They were like the "two up, two down" houses in British industrial areas that he had studied in college. He had them cheaply made, skimping on the insulation, using poor building materials, and cut-rate windows. But spruce them up with a nice paint job and the workers would never notice, reasoned William. Besides, once the truth of the construction of the buildings came to light, there would be nothing the workers could do about it. "The buildings only need to look good for a short time," laughed William.

In a relatively short time, William Franklin had secured six barns for his boatbuilding business, acquired the necessary tools and materials, and had his rowhouses for the new workers built and ready to go. He then headed for the docks in the New York area to recruit shipwrights for his newfound business. He went to New York and beyond for two reasons. First, he did not want to rile up other owners of nearby boatbuilding businesses to prevent repercussions over "stealing" their workers. Secondly, and most importantly, he did not want his new employees to be "too close to home." William's plan would be far more effective if the workers lived far from where they come from.

William's recruiting efforts were extraordinarily successful. He offered fifty percent more wages than what the builders were currently earning at their jobs. He also offered them "fine" housing at low rates and new tools and equipment to do their jobs. William had more takers than he had positions. He had only one requirement from his prospective employees; they would have to sign a six-month contract renewable based on the worker's performance. That was the setup in William's master plan. He would lose money in the short term, but more than make up for it in the long run.

William had all his new employees show up for work on April 1st, a fitting day for what he had in mind for his new workers. The new boatbuilders moved into the new rowhouses, most with their families, and work commenced the following day. They all had signed six-month contracts providing the employee with a generous wage and a rowhouse with low monthly rent. Additionally, because there were few retail stores in the surrounding area, company stores provided products at more than reasonable prices. And to top it off, the employee could walk away from the contract anytime. For the workers, it was too good to be true. It was!

For the first contract period things went very well. The men thought that working for William Franklin was the best thing that ever happened to them. But William made little profit after paying wages and providing benefits for his workers. He also made little profit selling his boats, although they had quickly built a reputation as one of the finest built boats on the market. That was soon about to change.

By the end of September, the terms of the first contract between William and the workers were about to expire. None of the workers he had hired left early, and they seemed happy with the work and conditions at the business. William had called a meeting with all the boatbuilders in one of the barns. He told them that the first contract was to expire at the end of the month and if the workers wanted to continue with their employment with him, a new contract would have to be signed. Everyone was happy with the wages they were receiving and the benefits of housing and low prices at the company stores so they were eager to sign new contracts.

However, these new contracts were not as generous, to say the least, as the first contract. William had hired a lawyer friend in Boston to write up his new employment contract for his workers. It was written in legalese, difficult for the boat workers to understand, but for a lawyer, very easy to manipulate the terms. For the employees, that was the good part. Buried under lawyer speak included a sneaky penalty tied to a term change: the term of the contract changed from six months to ten years. Besides death, there would be no easy way to break the contract without incurring a harsh financial penalty. The penalty clause stated that the employee would have to reimburse William for past wages and other benefits going back to the beginning of the first contract.

The contract also said that if the work building boats became unsatisfactory, the employee would be fired, and the conditions above would still apply to prevent any slowdowns or shoddy work. Moreover, William also had the right to raise the rent on the rowhouses at will, and to change the prices charged at the company stores. He had calculated that he would make loads of money and recoup his losses from his employees' first six-month contract. William had provided food and plenty of spirits for the meeting and explained the new contract to his workers.

He told them that the new contract would guarantee them ten years of employment with raises and their housing for the contract term. The "employer protections" segment of the contract was quickly glossed over. William offered his employees the contract to read so they could look it over before signing, knowing they would not understand the contract's language. William himself had a hard time understanding it and he knew what was in it. The workers, full of spirits and food and happy with how the last six months went, eagerly lined up to sign their contracts. A few were a little suspicious, but it was unanimous; they all signed up for the next ten years. The workers continued to celebrate their good fortune long into the night. William gathered up his newly signed contracts, smiling, and returned to his home to scheme for next month's bombshell. The date was September 27th. For the next three days, everything was fine. Then came October 1st.

On the morning of October 1st, William Franklin called his workers together. He brought up an "employer protection" he had put into the contract. William told the men that he would have to raise the rent charged for the rowhouses by ten percent due to unforeseen circumstances. This news was not well received by the workers and much grumbling and complaining was voiced over the increase. William assured the men that this was probably a one-time thing. That seemed to calm the workers a bit. However, it was not a one-time thing. The following six months brought four more rent increases. William even implemented one of those increases during the Christmas holidays. Another thing that angered the workers and their wives was the exorbitant price increases in the company stores that William had established. The builders worked six days a week and attended church on Sundays. This left little time for the employees and their wives to comparison shop elsewhere, not to mention the lack of transportation to far-flung stores elsewhere. Between the rent increases and the store prices, the boatbuilders were making less money than they did before they signed the new contract!

Some of the men slowed down construction or threated to quit but William explained that under the terms of the contract they would be liable for their wages and rent payable back to their original hiring date. A few workers tried disappearing in the night, but William had them arrested and they reluctantly agreed to come back to work.

Morale was low. The men started calling the area of the rowhouses "Rentham" due to the high rent and the shoddy buildings. William's plan for getting his money back was going as planned and he couldn't be happier.

The workers formed a committee to try and work this out with Mr. Franklin. It was led by John Sheldon. John and his wife Susan and their three sons were from New York. They were one of the first families to move to the area to build boats. Therefore, he knew every one of the workers well and was well-liked by the men. The committee met several times with William to work out an agreement to ease the stores' rent increases and prices. Despite their pleas, William wouldn't budge. He said that the contract is what it is, and the men should not have signed it if they didn't like the terms. John Sheldon sent a copy of the contract to his lawyer friend in New York and was told that the contract was valid and that nothing could be done about it. But something had to be done, because the rent increases and price increases were relentless, and at this rate, the men would be broke before the ten years were over. John was a smart and determined man and he vowed to find a solution to this problem. But how?

John agonized over this dilemma but could not find an answer. Then he got lucky. John's wife Susan attended a church meeting. She met the local teacher, Mary Kent, a septuagenarian who had taught at the town school for fifty-two years. Mary Kent had a keen memory and a sharp recollection of every student she had taught. In the conversation, Susan mentioned the troubles at the boat building business. Mary had heard of the problems and sympathized with Susan. She told Susan that they would have their hands full with William Franklin along with some specifics about the type of person he was. Mary said that the worst thing that happened to William was the death of his grandfather. Had he lived longer, perhaps William would have turned out differently, because he was the only person that could get through to William's humanity. Even on his deathbed, Mary recounted, the grandfather tried to straighten out William. He told William that if he didn't change his ways, he'd return from the dead to get him! Mary laughed. William's mother said her son was terrified and hadn't slept for weeks. Even today, William always slept with the light on at night "He's still scared of his grandfather coming back?" Susan asked. "Oh yes, definitely," Mary said. Susan couldn't wait to tell John.

That evening when John came home from work, Susan reprised the conversation she had with Mary Kent, including sharing the relationship William had with his grandfather and how William feared his grandfather coming back from the dead to get him. "Well, that's all well and good," said John, "but how does that help us?" Susan reminded John of the book A Christmas Carol and how Ebenezer Scrooge changed after ghostly visitations. "I remember and... I think I know where you're going with this," John said. Susan continued, "Why don't we pay a visit to William in the middle of the night?" John thought about it and said it was a crazy idea, but it might just work. Besides, at this point, what did they have to lose?

John and Susan met with the other workers to share their idea. Everyone agreed that it was a long shot but why not try it? John sent Susan back to talk to Mary Kent to get more information about the relationship between William and his grandfather. With that information, they met with their co-workers and devised a plan. They got the materials they would need to fabricate some items and finalized a schedule for each stage of the project to be perfectly timed. Now all they had to do was wait until dark.

It was 2:30 AM when John and the team headed for William's house. Through some careful reconnaissance, they knew what time William went to bed, that he slept with the window open and where they could sneak into the cellar to turn off the power to shut down the bedroom light. The power-off man snuck into the basement and waited ten minutes to pull the fuse. In the meantime, two men put a ladder up against the house so John could reach the second-floor bedroom. John had found a ship captain's coat and hat. Susan had draped John in a sheet and did a fantastic make-up job, including a fake beard that Mary Kent described William's grandfather as having. John looked positively ghostly!

John stood tensely at the top of the ladder waiting for the power to be turned off. The light in the bedroom suddenly went out and John lit the ship's lantern he was holding and climbed into the window. The men below pulled the ladder away. "This is it!" thought John, "ready or not!" He could see William by the dim light of the swinging lantern, asleep in bed. John began hollering.

"William! William Franklin! Wake up!" William sat up startled and called "What? Who's there?" John held the lantern near his face so William could see and said, "William, it is I, your grandfather." John could see William's face go white even in the dim light. He struggled to keep from laughing. "Wha, wha, what do you want?" quavered William. It was William's worst fear come to life.

John said, "I warned you long ago William, that if you did not change your ways and become a good person, I must come back to get you. You have been bad before, with the way you treated your parents and others, but what you have done recently is beyond that. What you have done to your workers is abominable. You are ruining those people's lives and I will not stand for it. Therefore, as I warned you, I will bring you back to the dead with me!"

William cowered in the bed and cried "No, please, grandfather, don't take me back. Please. Please. Give me another chance. I will change. I promise."

John walked toward the bed holding the lantern high and let out a bloodcurdling scream. "No please, please grandfather. Please!"

John grabbed William by the nightshirt and, yanking him out of the bed said forcefully, "Will you? Do you promise to change?"

William cried, "Yes, yes, I will. I promise I will."

"What will you do to change?" roared John.

"I will tear up the contracts," sobbed William, "I will make good for the men. I will. I promise I will." John let go of William's nightshirt, which flapped limply against his chest.

"William, I warn you, keep your promise. Next time you see me, you will be going with me."

"I will. I will," said William still cowering on the floor.

"You'd better for your sake," growled John. With one last blood-curdling shriek, John ran towards the window and went flying out of it and was deeply relieved when he saw the six men holding the canvas that he would tumble into. John landed in the canvas, the man in the basement put the fuse back in and they quickly disappeared into the night. The men headed back to "Rentham" and hoped their plan had worked. Meanwhile, William, sweating, pale, and visibly shaken, headed for his office.

The following day, William, looking haggard, called a meeting with all the workers. After bidding them "Good morning," he pulled out all the contracts from his briefcase and tore them up, one by one. He told the men that there would be no more contracts, and they all would get raises. They could leave anytime they want without repercussions. William also told them that the rowhouses would be repaired and refurbished. Moreover, he would gift his workers the houses and land so they could start their own town. He also lowered the prices in the company stores to reasonable prices. The cheers from the men were deafening. The workers could not believe the change in William, and they wondered how he could be so different in the span of one night. John, Susan, and the committee just winked at each other and smiled.

William was good to his word. His boatbuilding business was still thriving. Though he didn't make as much money as he planned, he didn't renege on his promise to the ghost of his grandfather . The townspeople and farmers were confused by his changed behavior, but he became popular and well-liked by all. The workers elected John and the committee to run their new town given to them by William. Their first act of business was to devise a name for the town. They decided on Wrentham. They thought adding a W to the name would sound a little classier. And in appreciation of John's leadership and Susan's great idea, the men all voted to also name the section of Wrentham where John and Susan's house was located; Sheldonville. Somewhere an old sea captain is smiling.

CHAPTER 9
New Braintree

Well, needless to say, you can probably guess how this small central Massachusetts town got its name. If you read how Braintree got its name, you know where this is going. I don't think we want to bring up all the gory facts of the Braintree story again. So, for propriety and good taste I'll give you the short version.

When the Commoners were discovered and attacked by the Plymouth militia, not everyone was gathered around the tree. Four Commoners were out in the woods acting as lookouts because they suspected that other soldiers were lurking in the underbrush. Undiscovered by the militia and with no chance to help the Commoners defeat the attackers, they decided to flee the area. They stealthily followed the militia back to Plymouth and saw The Leader and the others hung. The four Commoners decided to leave the region.

They hiked for weeks until they found an area that would later become the town. They settled in to resume their religious practice that began in England and continued at the Plymouth Colony. None of the four had the charisma of their former leader. They attempted to convert people they met when they ventured out and about, but got no takers. The four, with their twisted mindsets, took the rejections badly. They began kidnapping and killing people to hang the victim's brains on a tree at their camp.

They started slowly at first. A disappearance every 4 to 6 months or so. In time the abductions picked up. A couple of hunters came upon the Commoners' camp one day while they were out and saw the tree strewn with brains and hurried back to alert officials about what they found. People in the surrounding areas were terrified and sent word to Boston for help.

One of those officials in Boston was from Braintree and knew the story of how his town got its name. He was afraid that the same thing that happened years before was happening again. A group was formed and sent to the area where the disappearances were happening. The hunters showed them where they saw the tree, and the officials waited for the Commoners to return.

When they returned, the Commoners were captured and sent to Boston to stand trial, where they were convicted and hung for their crimes. As with Braintree, when settlers came and showed the town, it was decided to name the town New Braintree to honor the victims of the Commoners.

CHAPTER 10
Ware

Unlike all the other stories in the book, this one is true. It's not how the town of Ware got its name, but I think it's funny. So, with apologies to Abbott and Costello...

She grew up in the Midwest originally, and she was unfamiliar with many of the city and town names of Massachusetts. She was taking a call one day from a customer. When my friend asked the woman where she lived, the woman replied, "Ware."

"Where do you live?" my friend asked again.

"Ware," said the woman.

"Yes, where do you live?"

"Ware is where I live."

"I don't know where you live. That is why I am asking. Where do you live?"

"Yes, Ware. I live in Ware."

"Ma'am, I don't know where you live. That's why I am asking. If I knew, I wouldn't be asking."

"You don't understand. I live in Ware in Massachusetts."

"Ma'am, I can't help you if you don't tell me where in Massachusetts you live."

"I live in the town of Ware in Massachusetts."

"Ma'am, I am trying to help you, but I need this information to answer your questions so please, where do you live?"

The exchange continued in this vein until the woman said, "I live in the town called Ware. It is spelled W-A-R-E. It's a town in central Massachusetts."

My friend's co-worker heard this conversation and told her to put the call on hold. She explained to my friend that there is a town in Massachusetts named Ware. My friend apologized and continued to help the woman.

CHAPTER 11
Swampscott

You can likely guess how the town of Swampscott got its name and you would probably be right. But let's hear it anyway. The land that was to become Swampscott was originally part of the town of Lynn. It was settled in 1629, when the first Massachusetts Bay Colony tannery was built on Humphrey's Brook, a river that bordered a large marshy area. Fishing became a prominent industry in the budding town. There were shoemakers, farmers, and merchants, but fishing was the lifeblood of the townspeople. For years things were solid for the locals. It was a community of modest means, and everyone was able to make a living. However, things were about to change for the good people in this section of Lynn.

In 1754, unrest between British colonies and French colonies erupted from the Province of Virginia to Newfoundland Canada in the north. Each side was supported by various north American Indian tribes. It became known as The French and Indian War. The French colonists, numbering some 60,000 were vastly outnumbered by the two million British colonists but despite the disparity in numbers, the war dragged on for nine long years. Most of the fighting took place far from where our story takes place; however, there was an incident that proved potentially deadly for the inhabitants of our story.

Around 1756, rumors started circulating among the townspeople that the French were planning an attack to shut down the local fishing fleet, which would be a huge blow to the local economy. People were nervous about the rumors, but town leaders didn't think there was any substance to the talk, and urged the townsfolk to calm down and go about their business. After all, most of the fighting was in New York, Pennsylvania, and up north in Canada. The town leaders didn't want to take extra safeguards above their normal precautions. For example, any problems with the local Indian tribes had been few and far between in the past years. "No," thought the local leaders, "there is nothing to be worried about."

Well, as you probably guessed, there was something to worry about. Late in the fall of that year, a surprise invasion came from the French and caught the town completely unprepared. Just as dawn was breaking, the French came by sea in ships and attacked the fishing fleet and the town. Chaos resulted as people tried to figure out what was going on. Of course, there wasn't any organized response to the onslaught because the town leaders didn't think there was anything to worry about. Some shots were fired, but most people ran towards the woods on the outskirts of town to escape the attacking French. Unfortunately for the retreating townsfolk, two of the local tribes had been recruited by the French to help them raid the town and join in on the spoils.

As the people were running away from the town and French raiders, suddenly arrows were being fired at them from the Indians attacking from the woods in front of them. The townspeople were cut off by the French and the Indians, and the only avenue of escape was to race towards the tannery by Humphrey's Brook. And race they did, but there was still a problem. They had been so shocked by the attack that the townspeople hadn't had time to gather up enough weapons to hold off the invaders if they chose to make a stand in the tannery. It would be just a matter of time before they would be overrun. They could keep running but beyond the tannery and Humphrey's Brook lay marshes and swampland full of quicksand and mucky bogs filled with sticky mud and murky water. If the attackers didn't get them, the swampland would. Things looked bleak for the escaping townsfolk. As they ran towards the tannery with the French and the Indians in pursuit, they all spied a familiar figure standing at the swamp's edge.

The man standing at the swamp's edge was known to most of the townspeople. Most people guessed that he was around sixty years of age. His clothes were dirty and ragged. He would occasionally come to town and barter for what he needed with animal skins. He rarely spoke, only saying the minimum. When he finished his business, he would head back to the swamps. No one knew his name, but he was known as Scott. One of the old timers who had died a few years ago said that was his name, so they all called him that. Sure, some of the young children made fun of him and some of the more proper ladies and gentlemen of the town were appalled when he came to town, but most just let him be.

Scott watched, and wondered why the whole town was running towards him. He was about to run away, because he thought they were coming for him when he heard people yelling, "Run!"

"Help!"

"We're being attacked!"

"The Indians and the French are attacking!"

Scott waved his arms. "Come!" he yelled, "Follow me." He headed toward the swamp. The people running for their lives were apprehensive about following Scott into the marshes but there was little choice. "Step where I step!" Scott called out, "and tell people behind to do the same." Scott grew up and lived in the swamplands and he was acquainted with every inch of it. He knew both the high points of stable ground and rocks as well as the low points of every pool of mud and quicksand.

The fleeing group followed Scott into the swamp as quickly and carefully as possible. A rear guard formed from the few men with guns at the group's back. They tried to hold off the attackers while the rest fled after Scott. The French and Indian attackers tried to follow the townspeople into the swamp but quickly got stuck in the muck, pools of water, and quicksand, so they retreated from the swamp. The group followed Scott through the marshes until they all came out on the other side, which was remote part of Lynn. Some of the rear guards were killed, but everyone else survived thanks to the mysterious swamp man named Scott. Once all were out of the swamp, Scott waved to the group and called out, "You OK now?" and disappeared back into the swamp.

The townspeople called for Scott to return so they could thank him for saving their lives, but he did not reemerge from the trees. The escapees told the authorities what had happened. The militia counter-attacked days later and captured the French attackers and forced the Indians back into the woods so the people were able to return to their village. The war continued for some years, but there were no further attacks by the French or the Indians. Scott was never seen again after the day he helped them escape. Some thought that he was afraid of another attack. Others thought that maybe he was injured during the attack and perished. And a third opinion was that Scott died of old age. Whatever it was, Scott was never seen again after he saved the townspeople.

When the property became incorporated as a town separate from Lynn, there weren't any arguments over what to name the town. From the day the townspeople were saved by the marsh-dwelling hermit, the area was known as Swampscott.

CHAPTER 12

Dana, Enfield, Prescott, and Greenwich

We're going to depart a little from how towns got their names in this story. This tale is not about how these four towns got their names but what happened to them. If you look on a map of Massachusetts, you won't find these four towns. So let us find out where they are, ...er, where they were and what happened.

All four towns were once located in Central Massachusetts. They all pretty much bordered each other. All four were small towns, and each one had a church, small town hall, and a tavern. The population of each was a few thousand people or so. Most were farmers, a few tradesmen, and shopkeepers. Pretty typical of small towns in the mid to late eighteen hundreds. All except Greenwich were incorporated in the early eighteen hundreds. Dana was named after a famous political leader, Josiah Dana, a well-respected and reserved man, who owned a good part of the land and built the biggest house in town. Enfield got its name from one of its earliest founders, Scott Enfield. It was rumored that he had something to do with the Enfield rifle, which plays a part later in our story, but no one knew for sure. Prescott was named for Colonel Robert Prescott, a decorated army man who played a significant part in the Revolutionary war. Greenwich was started by British sympathizers in the mid seventeen hundreds who named it after the Duke of Greenwich. Not the most popular name for a town after the American Revolution but the name stuck. So that's how the four towns got their names. With that out of the way, let us move onto the "what happened?"

The story of our four towns' demise takes place in the nineteen thirties and involves the descendants of the towns' founders. In Dana, lawyer William Dana lived in his grandfather's house with his wife Martha and their twin sons, Jeffery, and Frank. Like his father and grandfather before him, William was well respected. Life was good for the Dana family, except…. Frank was a bit of a problem. The boys were eighteen years old, and Jeffery was a lot like his father, but Frank was a little wild. He had a mind of his own and didn't like being told what to do. In Enfield, we have Lee Enfield. Lee was a farmer and a widower with one daughter named Jean. She was eighteen years old and very comely, attracting the appreciative glances of many of the boys in the area. However, her father was very possessive and did not like boys sniffing around his daughter.

Over in Prescott we have Oliver Prescott. Oliver was also a farmer, married with seven children, five boys and two girls. The Revolutionary War never ended for Oliver. He still had a hatred of all things British, handed down from his grandfather and father before him and he passed that hatred down to his children. And the focus of that hatred was on the neighboring town of Greenwich. Now in Greenwich, despite not changing the town's name after the war, there were no obvious or hidden British sympathizers living in the town.

The town was named almost two hundred years ago, but hatred dies hard for some people, like Oliver Prescott. Harold Quabbin, a descendent of one of the men who originally named the town, lived in Greenwich. He was also eighteen years old and orphaned at an early age. He lived with the pastor of the town church and the pastor's wife. Harold constantly had problems with the Prescott kids. He also, like Frank Dana, was smitten with Jean Enfield. The children of the four towns all went to the same school centrally located on Prescott and Greenwich border, and all the children of the four towns knew each other.

So, let's recap before we continue the story. We have levelheaded Jeffery and impulsive Frank Dana, who wants to marry Jean Enfield. Then we have Oliver Prescott, and his kids who hate anyone from Greenwich. Next up is Harold Quabbin who also has strong feelings for Jean and is constantly tormented by the Prescott gang. Finally, the Enfields. Jean who likes both Frank Dana and Harold Quabbin, and her father who doesn't approve of anyone who admires his daughter. OK, we got that straight? Let's move on. Now I'm not going to go into forty-five different incidents between Harold and the Prescott gang, or Lee Enfield and Frank Dana, or Jean and Harold or Frank. You're not here for a three-hour story, so I will summarize the events leading up to the climax of our story.

Jean Enfield, like I said earlier, was a very pretty girl. She was likable enough. She got along with most people and enjoyed the boys' attention in school. She especially liked Frank for his personality, and she liked Harold for his sweetness. Because of her father's disapproval around courting , she sneaked around to see Frank and Harold because she was afraid of her father's rage if he happened to catch her with a boy. Lee Enfield was a decent man, but his wife's death had changed him. He had to bring up Jean alone, and at that time, he committed himself to raising and protecting his nine-year-old daughter to the point of fanaticism. Lee had an Enfield rifle by the fireplace, and Jean was afraid that he might lose his temper and use it one day. So, Jean was cautious when she met up with either Frank or Harold.

Now when it came to Frank, he was very bold with regards to Jean. He was bound and determined to marry her. He would wait for her right in the open when he went to her house to see her, show up at her window at night, and he would leave presents on her porch. Jean was left to make up stories about those presents to her father. Frank was trying to prove his love to Jean, but she feared he might get shot. He knew she didn't want to marry him, and that she also liked Harold. He couldn't see reason where she was concerned. All of his family tried to talk some sense into him, but Frank would not listen. He was going to marry Jean, and nothing would stop him from doing that.

Let us turn our attention to Harold Quabbin. Harold had two issues to deal with. One of course, was Jean Enfield. He had known Jean since they both were children. Harold had intense feelings for Jean, but he also knew she was ambivalent. He didn't like that Jean would see Frank but knew it didn't make any difference. Harold hoped that someday he and Jean would be together, and it hurt that he knew deep down in his heart that it would never happen. He loved her but it was not reciprocal. He and Jean were good friends, and that was where it would stay, or so he thought.

Harold had another big problem. The five Prescott boys. They were tough, and they were mean. They did not like anyone from Greenwich, but they particularly did not like Harold. Somehow, they found out that Harold was related to one of the town's originators. That put a big target on his back regarding the Prescott gang. Over the years there were multiple fights. More like beatings because Harold was always outnumbered by the Prescotts. Vandalism happened, and vile stories were spread about Harold being responsible. Harold got pretty good at avoiding the Prescott boys but with everyone getting older the trouble between them was ratcheting up.

Fortunately, the Prescotts didn't know about Harold's secret place. The four towns were set down in the Swift River Valley. Many years ago, men from the area built a dam on the river for to irrigate the valley's crops. The dam sat high, with a bird's eye vista of all four towns. Harold liked to climb up to the dam when he needed to think and get away from his problems. It seemed like Harold was spending more and more time up at the dam. Life was difficult lately with the pull and push of his feelings around Jean and Frank Dana, in addition to escalating problems with the Prescott boys. Harold was depressed, but unfortunately for Harold, things were about to get worse.

The Prescott boys were getting bolder and bolder with their unreasonable hatred of the town and the people of Greenwich. Part of the problem was that the boys were getting older and started drinking the moonshine their father made in the barn. Alcohol tends to make some people bolder with a tendency to do stupid things, which was the case with the Prescotts. After a tense meeting between with Harold in the schoolyard, the Prescott boys headed out to the woods with a big jug of their father's moonshine. The boys polished off a good part of the jug and in their drunken state, they decided to act on something they said during the argument in the schoolyard earlier that day. They would set fire to the church in Greenwich where Harold lived. It was already sunset, so they got what they needed from the barn and headed for Greenwich. It was dark by the time they got there. They sneaked up to the church and started several fires around the church. With that, the boys hightailed it back home, laughing about what they had done.

While that was happening, Harold had gone to visit with Jean. He and Jean met in the woods near Jean's house when Frank Dana appeared. Frank was jealous of Harold, and he was upset that she was with him. Frank got into a shouting match with Harold and Jean tried to quiet them down so her father wouldn't hear them. But the shouting and pushing spilled out into the front yard of Lee Enfield's house. Lee rushed to get his rifle by the fireplace. Meanwhile Frank and Harold were grabbing each other's shirt collars shouting at each other with Jean trying to get between them to break them up. It was just bad luck that the two boys were between Jean and her father because just as she pried them apart, Lee fired his rifle at them. Instead, the shot went right into his daughter's heart, and she died before she hit the ground.

Frank and Harold scattered in opposite direction, fearful of being shot by Lee Enfield. Lee was horrified by what happened and sobbed uncontrollably, cradling his dead daughter.

Harold couldn't believe what believe that the girl he loved was dead. What made it worse for Harold was that just before Frank showed up, Jean had told Harold that she loved him too, and wanted to get married if he would have her. It seems that Harold had misinterpreted their relationship all along. If Frank had not showed up when he did, he could have married Jean and moved away to start a new life. Now all that possibility was just a bloody corpse on the grass at the Enfield house. He ran as fast as he could back to Greenwich. Despite that tragedy, things were going to get a lot worse for Harold.

As he came upon the church and small house where he and the pastor and his wife lived, all he saw was the blackened remains of the two buildings. He instantly knew who was responsible for it. A couple of the residents that gathered around came over to Harold to tell him that the pastor and his wife had died in the fire. Upon hearing that news, Harold ran up to the dam to process the tragedies . He sat there thinking about all the tragic events that he just experienced. The girl who, his whole life, he thought was his unrequited love, told him that she wanted to be with him forever! Then that jerk Frank Dana shows up and causes Lee to accidently shoot his own daughter. The love of Harold's life! Then the Prescott boys, who had tormented him from childhood , burned his house down and killed the only parents he had ever known! The whole thing was just too much for Harold to bear. He decided that he did not want to live anymore. But he also wanted revenge. Revenge on those who ruined his life. So, he headed back to Greenwich.

It was about one in the morning, and everyone was asleep when Harold got back to town. He headed for the town storehouse where various items were housed including armaments. He gathered up as much gunpowder and dynamite that he could carry and headed back up to the dam. He made several trips between the storehouse and the dam. Harold packed all the dynamite and gunpowder at the base of the dam. Before he lit the fuses, he went to the hilltop overlooking the four towns. He thought about Jean and what might have been. But now Jean was gone forever. He thought about the pastor and his wife and how kind they were to him. But now they, too, were gone forever.

He thought about Frank and how he ruined what might have been. Yet he was still down there in Dana. He thought about Lee Enfield who shot the love of his life. Yet he was still down there in Enfield. He thought about the Prescotts and how they constantly tormented him most of his life. They burned down his house and killed his foster parents. Yet they were still down there in Prescott. All the good was gone and all the bad was still there. He hated the four towns! Harold did not want to live anymore but he was going to take the towns and the people who ruined his life with them. Harold cursed out loud at the towns and the people he hated, and as his screams echoed over the water, he lit the fuses.

The explosion was thunderous and shook the houses in all four towns. It was early in the morning and most people were either just getting up or still in bed. What people saw when they looked outside was a wall of water coming down the hill from where the dam used to stand. Some ran, some climbed on the roofs of their houses, some just stood there in disbelief. But there was nowhere to go. The water kept rising and rising. Soon, all four towns were submerged in the waters from the Swift River. Some townspeople survived. Some were quick enough to get away or had boats to clamber onto, but most perished in the newly formed lake.

The state authorities showed up a few days after the dam explosion to investigate what had happened. They found all four towns under water. They assisted the survivors after documenting and interviewing them. It turns out not everyone was sleeping when Harold was gathering the explosives that night. A couple of people saw him sneaking out of the storehouse, but they figured they would tell the police in the morning. The state authorities, through interviews about what had happened the night before, figured out that Harold had blown up the dam. They began calling the large new lake the Quabbin Reservoir. Maybe not the best name considering the circumstances but, like Greenwich, the name stuck. The city of Boston was looking for a new public water supply so at least some good came from the tragedy.

This was a cautionary tale about hatred gone awry and as unfortunate as it was, Harold was successful with his revenge: Frank Dana, Lee Enfield, and the Prescotts were never seen or heard from again.

CHAPTER 13
Seekonk

A bird graces the Town of Seekonk seal, and that bird is a goose, which plays a prominent role in our story of how Seekonk got its name. But first, a little history lesson. The earliest known inhabitants of Seekonk were Native Americans from the Wampanoag Tribe. When the colonists settled in Southeastern Massachusetts, the chief of the Wampanoags was known as Massasoit. Massasoit decided to make a peace treaty with the new immigrants. Perhaps the most important reason was that the Wampanoags feared being overtaken by the nearby Narragansett Indians. Massasoit believed an alliance with the English would help secure his people's safety. In 1641, the local Native Americans had granted a large part of modern-day Seekonk to purchasers from Hingham, including Edward Gilman Sr., Joseph Peck, John Leavitt, and others. In 1653 Massasoit and his son Wamsetto, (also known as Alexander to the English) signed a deed granting the land that is now Seekonk and the surrounding communities to Thomas Willitt, Myles Standish, and Josiah Winslow. The Wampanoags were paid 35 pounds sterling for the sale by Willitt, Standish, and Winslow.

Three of the first English men to settle in the area now known as Seekonk and Providence were William Blackstone, Roger Williams, and Samuel Newman. These men and their followers proved it was possible to provide a living away from the coastal areas. This allowed groups of individuals to separate themselves from Puritan control. This led to a greater diversity of culture, religious, and philosophical freedom. It was only by forming alliances with the Native Americans in both the Wampanoag and Narragansett tribes that these early settlements were able to flourish. Massasoit lived until he was 80 years old. While he lived, his people and the settlers lived in relative peace. He was followed in power by his son Wamsetto, also known as Alexander. Wamsetto died shortly after his father and was replaced by his brother Metacomet, also known as King Philip. In 1675, King Philip's War began and both sides saw this as an opportunity to claim the land for their people and their way of life. So now that we're up to speed with the historical backstory, let's find out about the goose and why it's on the town seal.

Before King Philip's war, William Shakley, one of the settlers in the area, known as Bill, did a little farming, raised some livestock and such, like most people did at that time. He had some chickens and geese. All the other farm animals were just animals, but one of the geese was special to him. This particular goose was much smarter than the other geese. He would follow Bill around and he would actually help Bill with some of the chores around the farm. Bill thought of the goose as his friend and named him Konk. It was a play on geese honking and, even though Bill loved the goose, sometimes the bird would drive him crazy, and he just wanted to conk the goose on the head. Bill didn't have a wife, family, or any other people on the farm, so he spent a lot of time with Konk. At the end of the day Bill would relax on his porch and chat with Konk, and to Bill's amazement, it seemed like the goose listened to and understood what Bill was saying. Bill would ask Konk a question and Konk would honk back an answer. It got Bill to thinking. He had heard that parrots could be taught to repeat phrases. Could Konk be taught to talk like a parrot?

Bill would spend every day talking to Konk while he worked and spent every evening trying to teach his goose how to talk. At first, the whole thing seemed fruitless, but then one evening Bill, after another frustrating night, said, "Konk, let's go to bed." Bill was shocked when he heard a honking voice answer, "No." Bill slowly sat down and went back to work teaching Konk to talk.

For the next six months, Bill was diligent about using his free time teaching his goose how to talk. He had taught Konk to say "yes," "no," "go away," "stop," and several other phrases. Bill showed Konk to some of the other farmers in the area. They were absolutely amazed at what they witnessed. "Imagine, a talking goose," they thought, "the money that could be made with a bird like that." Bill pondered whether he could make some money with Konk. So, Bill took to the road with his talking bird. He fixed up his wagon like the covered wagons you'd see in Westerns crossing the plain. He hung a big banner on both sides of the wagon that said, "COME ONE AND ALL AND SEE KONK THE TALKING GOOSE!" With that, Bill and Konk hit the road.

Bill traveled to many villages and towns near and far. He would charge a small fee to see Konk speak. People could not get enough of the goose; Bill would spend days in a town, and people would visit daily to see Konk again and again. All Bill would have to do is yell, "See Konk, see Konk," and Konk would walk out of the wagon and begin talking. The people would come running and hand over their money to see the talking goose. Bill was doing well moneywise with his talking goose shows, but traveling life was hard, and he missed his farm. Should he go back? But he was making so much money! What should he do? His mind was made up when he received a message…

…the message stated that the local Indians were uprising and encouraged him to return and protect his farm. Bill immediately packed up the wagon and headed back to the farm. When Bill returned, he met with the locals. He was told that Metacomet and his people had started attacking them to drive the farmers and their families away to reclaim the land. Now, King Phillip's War encompassed a large area throughout New England, but for this story, we're only concerned with the area where Bill and his neighbors' farms were located.

After many attacks by the Indians, things were looking bleak for Bill and the other farmers. The Indians had pushed everyone back to a corner on Bill's farmland. They surrounded the farmers at Bill's barn and were ready to attack when Bill, had a desperate idea. At this point, he thought, "What do we have to lose?" Bill yelled, "See Konk!" Konk came waddling out of the barn and honked, "Stop! Go away! Leave!" The Indians' faces went ashen, and they stared at the goose in disbelief. Bill started yelling and waving his arms with the other farmers joining in. Meanwhile, Konk kept walking toward the Indians, flapping his wings, and continued to honk, "Go away! Leave!" The Indians, believing that the goose was an evil spirit controlled by the farmers, turned and fled the area as fast as they could. The farmers cheered, and Bill opened his arms wide, and Konk flew into them for a big hug as the group marched around cheering. Konk, the goose, had saved them! Fighting raged on in nearby regions, but the Indians never came back to the area where Bill and the other farmers lived. The Indians eventually lost the war, and peace reigned.

When it decided to form a new town, the locals didn't forget who saved them from being slaughtered by the Indians; and they agreed to call the new town "Seekonk." The goose would be featured on the town seal to honor Konk, the goose who saved them during King Phillip's War.

CHAPTER 14
Needham

Y ou could look up the history of Needham to learn how the town was named, but I'm going to tell you the real story of how the town got its name. Let me introduce you to George Needham, who lived an exciting life. At age ten, young George became the cabin boy for a ship bound for South America. He was tortured by the captain and tattooed against his will. When the boat abandoned him on a remote shore in Brazil, he was captured by cannibal natives who wanted to eat him. After they peeled his clothes off like he was a banana, they became spooked by his tattoos and George escaped. As an adult, he became a preacher in England, traveling to spread the word in Ireland and New England. He continued his preaching tours to Japan, China and other places worldwide. He eventually settled in Dedham near Boston. But as fascinating as all this is, let's find out why the town was named after him.

George made a pilgrimage to the state of Maine at the behest of some of the preachers there. He traveled to the Portland area to lecture at some of the congregations of the surrounding towns. During his visit to Maine, he was asked to visit a local hospital and pray with the patients. He met and prayed with many patients, but one case particularly touched his heart. George met a nine-year old orphan, a little girl who was very sick, named Ruth Kelly. Shortly after her family moved from Ireland, the whole family was struck ill, and her parents died. Ruth rarely had visitors because she was alone in the world, but she was resilient and tried to make the best of her situation. After a year, her prospects of getting out of the hospital were not good. George spent a lot of time talking to Ruth. The nurses tried to give Ruth attention, but the hospital was poorly financed, and as a result, they were overworked and understaffed.

Ruth was happy to have someone to talk to, and she and George conversed for a long time. When he asked what Ruth missed most about Ireland, she told him that she missed the candy her mother used to make. He asked Ruth what kind of candy it was, and Ruth didn't know, but it was made with potatoes.

That raised George's eyebrows. "Potato? Are you sure your mother put a potato in the candy?"

"Oh yes," said Ruth, "I'm sure of it," she responded.

"Leave it to the Irish to put potatoes in candy," thought George with a smile.

"I would love to have some of my mom's candy again," said Ruth, "I haven't had candy since I came to the hospital." George and Ruth continued to chat until it was time for George to go.

He impulsively told Ruth, "I will try to bring you some potato candy when I come to visit you again." Ruth was so excited not just for the prospect of her favorite treat, but also for the promise of more company.

"How," thought George, "will I make this potato candy?" He was stumped. George went to the library and researched candy making and queried nearby candy makers on the subject. No one had ever heard of potato candy. George was at a crossroads. He didn't know how to make the candy, but he didn't want to disappoint Ruth. George decided there was only one thing left to do: experiment in the kitchen.

George borrowed the kitchen of a local pastor's wife. He tried many different combinations of ingredients to make the candy. None were quite right, and some were downright awful. Finally, George hit on the right combination. He boiled, then mashed the potatoes without milk or butter. He mixed the mash with powdered sugar, vanilla, shredded coconut, and a little bit of salt. Then he spread the mixture into a pan and cut it into squares. George then took each square and coated it with chocolate. He then tried one. "Wow!" he thought, "these are pretty good!" George called the pastor and his wife to the kitchen to try his potato candy. They both thought it was great. After trying the candy out on a few other people, George was ready to take the candy to Ruth. He was hoping that it was what Ruth's mother used to make for Ruth.

George arrived at the hospital the following day. He headed right for Ruth's bed. George thought to himself, "How sad she looks." He hoped that she would like his candy and that it would cheer her up. "Hello Ruth, how are you feeling this morning?"

Ruth opened her eyes and said, "Hello, Mister Needham. I'm OK." "Please call me George," he told Ruth. "OK… George."

"I've got a surprise for you," he told Ruth, "I hope you like it."

Ruth wondered what it could be. George pulled out a box from his bag. Ruth sat up and took the box from him, opening the lid. Her eyes grew wide, and a smile beamed across her face. "It's candy!" she squealed. "It's not just candy, Ruth. It's potato candy. I just hope it's like the candy your mother used to make." Ruth picked a piece of candy out of the box and examined it before taking a bite. As she chewed it, her face and eyes lit up. "It's just like the candy my mom used to make. It tastes the same. Where did you get it? I just love it." George explained to Ruth how he came to make it, but she only half listened, because she was enjoying the taste of the candy so much. George was amazed at how different Ruth's demeanor was after getting the candy. He hoped that his candy might be the spark Ruth needed to get well again. George told her he'd bring more candy in a couple of days. She was excited to hear that and couldn't wait until he visited again.

George had hoped that the potato candy would lift Ruth's spirits, but he couldn't have envisioned how well it did work. It proved to be the motivation that Ruth needed; within a few weeks, she was well and ready to leave the hospital. The problem was as an orphan, Ruth had nowhere to live, so George decided to take Ruth back to Dedham to find a friendly family that Ruth could live with rather than leave her in Maine. She had been through so much already, and he wanted Ruth to be happy, and he'd do his best to help.

Shortly after George and Ruth arrived back in Dedham, George began interviewing families to adopt Ruth. As luck would have it, George found one of the most influential families in town was open to adopting a child, since they could not have one of their own. George brought Ruth to meet the family. George brought Ruth to meet the family, and George told them her story and how the candy helped make her well again. Ruth and the family got along, and Ruth was soon adopted.

Now I know what you are thinking. So how did the town of Needham get its name? Well, Ruth's new family delighted in their new daughter, —you could say that it changed their lives. About a year after the adoption, the people in the section of Dedham where they lived decided that they wanted to become a separate town. When it came to naming the new town, Ruth's new family held a lot of sway over the matter and decided to call the town after its most celebrated citizen and who saved their new and beloved daughter Ruth. And that celebrated citizen was of course, George Needham.

A side note to the story, if you're ever in Maine, you'll find some stores that still sell the candy. They're called Needhams.

CHAPTER 15

Carver

T he town of Carver borders Plymouth. You may have read about the strange happenings in Plymouth described in another story in this book, but Carver has its share of those too. Carver was settled about twenty years after the Pilgrims landed in Plymouth in 1620. It was a typical village for its day. Mostly farms, a church, and some businesses. Life was quiet and uneventful. Everyone knew each other although they lived a good distance from each other back in those days. An unfortunate thing in light of the story I am about to tell.

Our story takes place in the 1750's. As said before, prior to the 1750's, the area was largely agricultural. In the 1740's, iron ore was discovered in the swamplands on the southern part of the budding town. Soon a few mills sprang up and that iron ore was put to good use. Many items were made in the mills but the primary products that were made were cooking utensils. Pots, pans, cutlery, and such. With the mills gearing up, more people were needed to do the work. It brought many people to the area to fill the jobs. The longtime residents were not pleased about all this. The farmers liked the way things were, and they were concerned about the quality of life and the trouble that would follow with all these new people coming to the area.

The new workers lived near the mills. There was not a lot of interaction between the farmers and the newcomers except where everyone overlapped at the stores, church, and tavern. There would be the occasional disagreement or fight at the tavern but otherwise, life went on without too many problems between the two groups. Most of the problems stemmed of the dislike of the mill owners by the locals, particularly Mr. Morris who owned the biggest mill in the area. There was a genuine dislike between the worried farmers and the combative Mr. Morris.

As I said earlier the farmers lived a good distance from each other so it would be days and sometime weeks with them not seeing each other. The talk at church on this particular Sunday was that no one had seen the Smith family in a while. This was the second Sunday that they hadn't been to church, and no one could recall seeing them anywhere else recently. It was decided that a couple of locals would check up on the Smith family after Sunday dinner. Two of the local men met up and headed for the Smith family farm. What they found made the two men wish they hadn't had dinner before going to the Smith farm. Upon entering the house, they found the entire family dead. Mr. and Mrs. Smith and their three children were dead and dismembered, body parts strewn throughout the house. It was a gruesome sight! Stuck in the middle of the kitchen table was a big kitchen knife. The men inspected the knife and saw that it had the Morris Co. insignia on it. It came from the Morris Company mill which was the biggest in the area.

After the men went back and informed the authorities about what they found, an inspection of the crime scene was conducted. It was discovered that the Smith family did not own any products from the Morris mill. It was thought that the murderer brought the knife with him before he killed the family. No motive could be found for the deed. Mr. Smith was one of the more vocal opponents of the mills and the new people it attracted to work in them, but other than that, no other motive made any sense.

It was about a month after the Smith murders when people noticed the Jones family hadn't been seen in a while. When they went to check on the Jones family's well-being, a similar scene awaited them when they entered the house. The family of six were found in various rooms of the house. Just like the Smith family, they were cut up and stabbed repeatedly and just like before, a Morris Company carving knife was stuck in the kitchen table. It was a sickening crime, and the authorities and local farmers were determined to find the killer or killers of the two unfortunate families.

A meeting was held with the residents, mill owners, and local authorities to figure out an action plan. A neighborhood watch would be set up to keep an eye out and to check on the farm families regularly. The farmers thought it was a good start, but they wanted more investigation of the mills and their employees. After all, this all started after the mills were built and their staff were hired. The mill owners said they would investigate their workers to see if any of them could be suspects in the crimes. Mr. Morris seemed agitated, because he didn't like the scrutiny he was getting from the locals, especially after the troubles he had from them when he was setting up his business. Yes, one of his company's knives was found at both crime scenes, but he wasn't responsible for the murders. Both victims were vocal critics of Mr. Morris, and he didn't like the insinuation that he or anyone working at his company was involved in them. The meeting ended although uncertainty lingered.

Over the next six months, four more murders happened in the village. All four followed the same MO as the first two. Brutal stabbings, dismemberment, and a Morris Co. knife stuck in the kitchen table. The only difference with these four murders was that the letter M was carved on the foreheads of the victims. This served to heighten suspicions against the Morris Company. The villagers were convinced that the killer worked at the company. They demanded that the authorities investigate or even shut down the company. They wanted "The Carver" as they called the murderer—because of the way the bodies were carved up— caught, and hung.

The investigations into the murders continued for months and years. So did the protests over the Morris Company mill, because the villagers were convinced that The Carver worked there. Despite scrutiny of the employees of the Morris mill, no suspects were arrested for the horrible deeds. Unfortunately, the murders continued. Three more happened in the following year, and five more in the next two years even though watch patrols were instituted, and everyone was on high alert. All the murders had the same characteristics. Carved up bodies, the letter M cut into the forehead of the victims, and a Morris Co. knife stuck into the table. Another common factor was that all the victims had been vocal critics of the mills, and especially of the Morris Company. This fact started to dawn on people. Outside of the murders, the mills had not changed the farmer's lifestyles all that much. Nevertheless, complaining and making life hard for the owners and employees of the mills, the farmers had hoped to convince them to pull up stakes and move or put them out of business. Mr. Morris and the other owners often opposed these attempts to ruin their businesses.

The farmers held another meeting. Because they were no closer to catching The Carver than when the first murders started, the farmers decided that the best course of action was to stop the protesting and harassment of Mr. Morris and the mill owners. It seemed clear that anyone who griped ended up a victim of the killer. No other ideas were forthcoming, and the farmers gave it a try. So, despite all the carnage over the past years, everyone just let it lie, kept quiet, and minded their own business.

Luckily for everyone, the killings stopped. The plan to leave the mill owners alone seemed to work. Years went by and The Carver hadn't returned. Speculation abounded on who the killer was and why the murders stopped. All seemed to think that the killer had been a mill employee, most likely a Morris mill employee since a Morris Co. knife was always found at the crime scene, and he must have decided to stop when he felt his job was no longer in danger becaused farmers stopped protesting the mills. As much as everyone wished that The Carver would be caught and made to pay for his heinous crimes, the authorities were no closer to catching him than they were after the first murder. It looked like The Carver would never be caught.

A number of years passed, and the influential men of the area decided to incorporate and become an official town instead of a part of Plymouth. Meetings were held to implement the process. When it came to naming the new town, the usual disagreements occurred. Everyone had their own idea on what that name should be. One of the most influential and successful of the men was Mr. Morris. He was bound and determined to name the new town after himself. After all, his highly successful mill had put this area on the map so to speak. Mr. Morris wanted to name the town Morrisville. Even though he was respected by the rest of the attendees, they didn't like the name. They wanted something else. Mr. Morris then suggested another name for the new town. He said that the name should be Carver. The other men instantly liked the idea of naming the town Carver. They said that it was a splendid idea to name the town Carver in honor of the first Governor of the Plymouth Colony. Mr. Morris smiled broadly and said "Of course!" …Well, it looks like Mr. Morris got his wish after all!

CHAPTER 16
Blandford

B landford is a town located in Hampton County. Blandford was first settled around 1732 mostly by settlers from Scotland. It was officially incorporated in 1741. Because of these Scottish families, Blandford was originally called "New Glasgow" after Glasgow, Scotland, but was renamed "Blandford" at the time of incorporation. Why was it changed from New Glasgow, which the settlers wanted, to Blandford? That's why I'm here to tell you the story.

Like I said, the area was settled around 1732. The town grew quickly and by 1740, the town decided to incorporate. The hopeful town fathers met and sent the petition to incorporate their town by the name of New Glasgow. The province of Massachusetts had recently appointed a new governor. When the town incorporation request was sent to Boston, the governor wanted to visit the prospective town. This would be the new governor's first official visit in the capacity of his new appointment, and he had high expectations. Being the highest government official, he expected a celebratory welcome. Perhaps a parade. Something befitting his position. The new governor was a pompous man and unfortunately for him, he was soon to be disappointed.

With anticipation of a glorious welcome by the residents, the governor and his entourage made the journey to the prospective town. When the governor arrived, with high expectations, he was immediately disappointed. There were no banners, parade, cheering crowds or bands playing. He was also struck by the ordinariness of the buildings, and of the church. No central town common. Through the critical, piercing eyes of the governor, it was a very bleak place. Now to be fair to the residents of the town, the new governor was an aristocrat and used to the finer things in life and this was his first trip outside of Boston to the countryside of Massachusetts. New Glasgow was not much different than many other towns in the western part of Massachusetts. Unfortunately for the residents of New Glasgow, being on the roster as first visit of a governor who knew little of the land west of Boston, they were to become "victims of circumstance."

The governor met with the town officials, and they presented him with the documents to become New Glasgow. After an underwhelming dinner and boring night in one of the resident's home, the governor headed back to Boston in the morning. As he rode out of town in his carriage, he turned to his lead assistant, nose high in the air , and said, "That had to be the blandest town I ever visited in my life."

When the governor returned to Boston, he had his staff process the papers to incorporate the town he had just visited. He did make one change to the application. He changed the name of the town from New Glasgow to Blandford.

The name change came at a cost to the townspeople. The people of Glasgow, Scotland, had promised the settlers a gift of a church bell if they named the town after their city. With the town now named Blandford, the bell was never sent. Today, Glasgow Road near the center of Blandford remains a silent reminder of these events.

CHAPTER 17
Shelburne Falls

S helburne Falls is a village between the towns of Shelburne and Buckland in Massachusetts. Although it's not a city or a town, it still has a fun backstory. This tale takes place in approximately 1834, at the time, Shelburne Falls didn't exist. The land that would become Shelburne Falls sat between Shelburne and Buckland. From 1779 onward, the land had been in dispute between two town founders: William Shelburne, who founded the town of Shelburne in 1768; and Mathias Buckland, who established the town of Buckland in 1779.

William Shelburne was an Irish-born politician from England who emigrated to America around 1756. He was a wealthy man who came to America to escape the pressures of British politics. He wished to settle down to the quiet, rural life that his father and grandfather had lived in England. William's father pushed him to change his life and not to settle for being a farmer like him and his father before him. William became a successful politician and accumulated wealth, but he missed the carefree rural life he had as a boy. He tried to reside in the in the English countryside, but he was constantly hounded by people seeking to use him for his influence.

He finally decided to go to America, where he was not well known to enjoy some peace and quiet. After arriving in Boston, where he was still recognized, he quickly moved to the western part of the state. He settled in the area where he would become a founder of a town named after himself. William used his wealth to construct public buildings and helped bring business to the region. The town would be incorporated in 1768; however, not all its land was included. The western part of the settlement was in dispute, so the state would only allow the residents to incorporate the eastern half of the settlement as the town of Shelburne. Do you want to know why? This is where Mathias Buckland comes in.

Mathias Buckland lived on the western half of the land bordering the settlement of Shelburne. Mathias had settled there years before William Shelburne or anyone else in Shelburne arrived. The land where Mathias and the other settlers lived was known as "No Town." They were frequently approached by representatives of the nearby villages of Charlemont and Ashfield to join them to help expand their towns but Mathias and the others who lived in No Town were not interested. Besides, Mathias had his hands full with the settlers in Shelburne. The residents of Shelburne wanted "No Town" land, which they thought they had rights to, to become part of Shelburne, but Mathias was adamant that the land belonged to No Town. When Shelburne began to incorporate, Mathias went to Boston to fight for the land of No Town to remain separate. The state ruled that the eastern part of the settlement of Shelburne could become a town, but the western section was in dispute and would have to be settled in the future.

The arguments over the land persisted for years with no resolution. Mathias and the settlers of No Town decided that they should incorporate as a town and finalize claims to the disputed property. They petitioned the state and became the town of Buckland in 1779, since it primarily was Mathias Buckland's idea. However, as with Shelburne, the state refused to let the disputed land between Buckland and Shelburne become part of Buckland. When the residents of both towns complained, they were informed by the state of Massachusetts that they must work out the boundaries themselves.

Unfortunately, without state involvement, the stalemate became a Hatfield and McCoy scenario. Gunshots and fistfights would become an everyday event between the residents of the two towns, and the feud went on endlessly for years. When William Shelburne and Mathias Buckland died, their sons Edgar Shelburne and Edward Buckland carried on with the war. The disputed land was fought over for fifty-five years, and the senseless deaths mounted. People on both sides, weary of the fighting and fatalities, were finally ready to end the conflict.

After much discussion, Edgar Shelburne and Edward Buckland determined to meet face to face and resolve once and for all, which town would lay claim to the land between Buckland and Shelburne. As you might have guessed, little progress was made to resolve the disagreement as the discussions droned on, with neither side willing to compromise. It was looking bleak. Suddenly, a ray of light appeared. During a break, Edgar and Edward, both horse connoisseurs, began bragging about their respective racehorses, shifting their argument from land boundaries to whose horse was fastest. They found a solution to the land dispute sparked by the debate about whose horse was fastest. Edward Buckland was certain that his horse was the best, and he challenged Edgar Shelburne to a horse race to decide whose horse was the fastest. The winner would claim the disputed property. Edgar was positive that his horse couldn't be beat, and he quickly accepted. There was much rejoicing in both towns that finally, an end to the feud was in sight.

After much anticipation, the big day arrived. It was a beautiful Sunday afternoon and after church, townsfolk from both sides gathered on the land between Buckland and Shelburne. No one from either town wanted to miss the end of the five-decade feud. Guns were prohibited so everyone felt safe as they lined up, flanking the finish line of the five-mile course. Each town was confident that their man and horse would win. Cheers rang out as Edward Buckland and his horse Thunderbolt appeared. The residents of Shelburne were not to be outdone when they roared at the arrival of Edgar Shelburne atop his horse Lightning. The two racers brought their horses to the start line, and the spokesman motioned for the crowd to settle down. He announced the two racers, their horses, and the terms of their bet. The first rider to cross the finish line would take possession of the disputed land for their town.

A bugler blew his horn to start the race. Both contestants lined up their horses, awaiting the start. The spokesman stood in front of and in between the horses holding a flag high in the air. The crowd seemed to quietly tense with breathless anticipation as they watched the flag gently waving in the breeze. The flag suddenly dropped, and the two horsemen raced off, hooves pounding in a drumbeat accompaniment to the crowd's roar. The horses quickly disappeared around the first bend, and the spectators knew that they wouldn't see them again until they came around that same bend heading home. There were observers along the course from both towns to ensure the competitors followed the race rules. The observers and the crowd alike were on pins and needles, waiting for the outcome of the big race.

It seemed like hours, but only a few minutes had passed when the lead horse came into view of the onlookers. Edgar's horse Lighting was the first around the bend, and a roar came from the Shelburne supporters. Edgar had a sizable lead on Edward Buckland and Thunderbolt, and there was no doubt that Edgar Shelburne would win the race. Edgar waved to his supporters. Edward Buckland urged his horse to run as fast as possible, but he knew he had lost the race. But fate is a funny thing. And as fate would have it, just as Edgar was waving and celebrating his apparent win to the crowd, his horse stumbled, and Edgar flew over Lighting's head and fell to the ground. He jumped up to leap into the saddle to finish the race, but was left looking on hopelessly as Edward and his horse thundered past him to the finish line. The Buckland residents roared, and the Shelburne townsfolk groaned at the sudden turn of events. The Buckland supporters headed back to their town to celebrate the win. Official announcements would be made the next day in a ceremony, finally ending the decades-long dispute by transferring the land rights.

After the celebratory party in Buckland, Edward sat in the living room of his house that night, contemplating the day's events. Because he won only by an act of fate, not by the fastest horse, he worried about the feud resuming, despite being able to claim the land by rights. He mulled over his options, but he was weary from the excitement of the day, and he decided he would think about it more later.

The next day Edward was having breakfast and picked up the newspaper off the kitchen chair to read about the big race from the day before. As he read the headline in big black letters at the top of the page, an idea popped into his head. A solution to the previous night's worries might be possible.

At the land transfer ceremony, jubilant Buckland and dejected Shelburne townspeople were in attendance. Both Edward Buckland and Edgar Shelburne were on the stage. Edgar Shelburne congratulated Edward and the town of Buckland on their win and confirmed that he and the town would honor the terms of the race agreement. Then Edward took the stage. He accepted Edgar's congratulations and expressed hope for an end of hostilities between the two towns. He went on to say that he felt unworthy of the win because Edgar was clearly going to win the race had his horse not stumbled and allowed Edward to win. Edward said that he was tired of the fighting over the land and because of the nature of his win over Edgar, hostilities might spill over again.

Edward therefore proposed an alternative to Buckland taking possession of the disputed land. Instead, he requested that the property between the two towns become a separate village, lived in by people from both towns. The crowd cheered and the residents from both towns shook hands with each other, celebrating the end of the feud with a win for both towns. When the noise died down, Edward told the crowd that as the winner of the race, he felt that he should be the one to name the new village. With that Edward held the newspaper headline high that he was reading that morning. He announced the name of the new village between Buckland and Shelburne, Shelburne Falls.

CHAPTER 18
Middleborough

Middleborough was incorporated as a town a long time ago. So why Middleborough? "Middle" isn't the name of a person or some big event. Well, let's find out.

The area that would become Middleborough was first settled in 1661 and known as Nemasket. Nemasket was the family name of one of the first and most important of the original settlers. John Nemasket came from England and first settled in Plymouth before striking out on his own. John and his wife Mary had three sons, William, George, and Joseph. The advantage of being one of the first families to settle in the region, allowed them to obtain a big parcel of land, which John named "Nemasket" after himself. As John Nemasket was the most important man in the area, the settlers decided that was a good name for the settlement.

Life was good for the Nemasket family except for George. John Nemasket always elevated his oldest son William to the detriment of his other two sons. When John spoke to other people it was always about William. On the other hand, Mary was always doting on her youngest son Joseph. He was a sickly child, and Mary was very protective of him. That left George, the middle child, to take care of himself. He was always lonely and felt left out of family matters because his father always spent time with William, and his mother was always giving care to Joseph. Life can be tough sometimes for the middle child.

As the years passed, nothing seemed to change. Even the other settlers were always preoccupied with John and William, or Mary and Joseph.

George was always the forgotten one. He grew resentful of his family and the other people in the settlement. He swore that some-day, somehow, he would get even with them.

As time went on, John grew old and feeble. Around this time, the settlers petitioned the state to incorporate and become a town. John's son William was chosen to lead the effort to incorporate. As usual, George wanted to help with the effort but was brushed aside by William and the others. "You're just the second son," he was told. "I'm the first born and I will run this endeavor," said William. On the other side, his mother had to spend all her time taking care of her husband and Joseph, who was never quite right and needed constant supervision.

As faith would have it, just before the papers were drawn up, William suffered a logging accident while clearing some land and died from his injuries. John had drawn up legal papers years ago saying that William would oversee his affairs if he became incapacitated, which was the reason William was handling the incorporation of the town. Now that William had died in the logging accident, legally according to the papers that his father had drawn up, George was next in line. Since it was stated in the legal papers, George was in charge and there was nothing anyone could do about it.

George felt good that for once he wasn't the forgotten middle child and was the important son now. As he filled out the forms to incorporate the new town, he scratched out the name Nemasket and filled in the new name that he decided to name the town. George wrote the name Middleborough on the town name line. The curse of the middle child was over.

CHAPTER 19

Quickie Tall Tales

Grampa, how did...

...Georgetown get its name?
  There were a lot of people named George in it.

...Belchertown get its name?
  Every year they used to have a big burping contest.

...Stoneham get its name?
  It's where they used to stone condemned prisoners to death.

...Harwich get its name?
  There was a witch who lived there and saved the town.

...Westminster get its name?
  English sympathizers lived there.

...Montague get its name?
  They defeated the Capulets.

...West Stockbridge get its name?
  It was west of Stockbridge.

...Shrewsbury get its name?
  It's where they put all the unruly women in the state.

...Barnstable get its name?
  They had a lot of horses there.

...Blackstone get its name?
Magicians like to live there.

...Lakeville get its name?
There's a lot of lakes there.

...Marshfield get its name?
The land is very swampy.

...Oak Bluffs get its name?
The trees there like to play poker.

...Rockland get its name?
Otherwise known as Ireland West.

...Salisbury get its name?
They eat a lot of steak there.

...Orange get its name?
They don't like apples there.

...Monroe get its name?
It has something to do with a girl named Marilyn.

...Great Barrington get its name?
They have a high opinion of themselves.

...Duxbury get its name?
Simple. A lot of ducks live there.

...Marblehead get its name?
Do I really have to explain that?

...Pepperell get its name?
It sounds better than Salterell.

...Wareham get its name?

There was a strong northwest wind blowing on the day of the explosion in Raynham.

...Sandwich get its name?

No, I can't be that obvious.

...West Roxbury get its name?

It must be because west is more popular than east. There are eight West-somethings in Massachusetts compared to only three East-somethings.

ACKNOWLEDGMENTS

I would like to take this opportunity to thank a few people who made this book possible. I mentioned them briefly in the forward but they need to be acknowledged for without them, this book would have never happened.

Firstly, I would like to thank my children Kristin, Michael, and Andrea. If it weren't for trying to entertain them on long car rides with these crazy stories when they were little, there'd be no tall tales, hence, no book. Never thought I would say this but, thank you for being fussy and cranky on those car trips.

Secondly, I would like to thank Evelyn for suggesting that, after listening to a couple of stories, I write a book of them. That thought never entered my mind.

Thirdly, a BIG thank you to my clerk, and more importantly my good friend Michelle, who, once hearing the idea of writing a book of these stories, provided me with endless encouragement to write the book and information on making it happen. Thank you Fluff, if it weren't for you, I would have never done it!

Fourthly, I want to thank Karyn my editor, for doing a great job for believing in my stories and producing this book.

And last but certainly not least, my wife Laurel who puts up with all my crazy ideas. It's been quite a ride so far!

www.ingramcontent.com/pod-product-compliance
Lightning Source LLC
Chambersburg PA
CBHW021932170626
46807CB00007B/3072